Low Midnight

A Kitty Norville Novel

CARRIE VAUGHN

A TOM DOHERTY ASSOCIATES BOOK
NEW YORK

This is a work of fiction. All of the characters, organizations, and events portrayed in this novel are either products of the author's imagination or are used fictitiously.

LOW MIDNIGHT

A Tor Book
Published by Tom Doherty Associates, LLC
175 Fifth Avenue
New York, NY 10010

www.tor-forge.com

Tor® is a registered trademark of Tom Doherty Associates, LLC.

ISBN 978-0-7653-6869-0

Tor books may be purchased for educational, business, or promotional use. For information on bulk purchases, please contact the Macmillan Corporate and Premium Sales Department at 1-800-221-7945, extension 5442, or write to specialmarkets@macmillan.com.

First Edition: January 2015

Printed in the United States of America

0 9 8 7 6 5 4 3 2 1

Praise for the Kitty Norville Series

"Fresh, hip, fantastic—a real treat!"
—L. A. Banks on *Kitty and The Midnight Hour*

"With the Kitty series, Vaughn has demonstrated a knack for believable characters . . . and mile-a-minute plotting."
—*Sunday Camera* (Boulder, CO)

"Do you like werewolves? Vampires? Talk radio? Reading? Sex? If the answer to any of those is yes, you're in for a wonderful ride."
—Gene Wolfe on *Kitty and The Midnight Hour*

"Fans of Vaughn's series will devour this and be ready for more."
—*Booklist* on *Kitty in the Underworld*

"Vaughn's universe is convincing and imaginative."
—*Publishers Weekly* on *Kitty Takes a Holiday*

"A fun, fast-paced adventure for fans of supernatural mysteries."
—*Locus* on *Kitty and The Midnight Hour*

"Suspenseful and interesting."
—*The Denver Post* on *Kitty's House of Horrors*

TOR BOOKS BY CARRIE VAUGHN

Kitty Goes to War

Kitty's Big Trouble

Kitty's Greatest Hits

Kitty Steals the Show

Kitty Rocks the House

Kitty in the Underworld

Low Midnight

Kitty Saves the World (forthcoming)

Discord's Apple

After the Golden Age

Dreams of the Golden Age

For all the readers who've been waiting for this one.

Low Midnight

Chapter 1

CORMAC SAT quietly while the man across the desk from him talked.

". . . model parolee, Mr. Bennett. I'm almost sorry to see you go." Porter gave a pleasant, practiced smile. He didn't mean anything by it. He was nondescript, a middle-aged bureaucrat with a plain suit and a tie someone else probably picked out for him. The office was equally nondescript, fifteen-year-old interior design washed out by fluorescent lights shining through frosted plastic. Cluttered desk, cluttered bookshelves, no view visible through a narrow window. Porter's padded executive chair didn't look much more comfortable than Cormac's hard plastic one. How'd the guy come here to work every day without going crazy? Cormac was itching to leave and never look back.

He tried a tight-lipped smile in return, because it was expected. It was polite, pretending like he thought the joke was funny. He kept his hands in his lap and twirled a braided band of leather wrapped around his right wrist. One turn, two, three . . .

Porter relaxed further, the vague look in his eyes suggesting he might actually have been enjoying himself. "Is there anything else I can do for you, Mr. Bennett? Anything at all?" He needed to be helpful, did Mr. Porter.

So many favors Cormac might ask for. Special grants for ex-cons, maybe some cash rewards, payouts. Request a full pardon from the governor, get his conviction overturned entirely, wipe the record clean and reinstate his concealed carry permit—

A bird in the hand, murmured a voice in the back of his mind. A woman's voice, speaking in an aristocratic English accent. *Let's not get carried away. It's enough to be done with this place.*

Cormac agreed. Stick to the plan, and the plan was to end his parole as quickly and painlessly as possible. Then stay the hell out of trouble so he'd never have to go through anything like prison again.

"No, sir," Cormac said. "I can't think of anything. Just your signature and I'll get out of your hair."

"That'll be my true pleasure, Mr. Bennett." Pen scratched on paper, the official document that meant Cormac was well and truly—finally—done with the Colorado Department of Corrections. He kept turning the braided cord, counting. Anyone watching would think he was fidgeting out of nervousness.

At last, Porter turned the pages around, showed Cormac the places he needed to sign, separated duplicate copies, folded one set, stuck them in an envelope, and handed the whole batch over.

"There you go. You are now what we call 'off paper' and officially out of the system. Congratulations."

The envelope should not have felt like a piece of solid gold in Cormac's hand, but it did. He should run. Flee, before Porter changed his mind.

Give the cord another turn or two, his ghost Amelia said. *Just in case.*

He did, fidgeting. Porter's expression was expansive, pleased. The man was so happy to help, wasn't he? He reached out to shake Cormac's hand. "Good luck, son."

Maybe they didn't need the spell to ensure Porter's cooperation. Maybe the wheels of justice didn't need any greasing at all on this end. On the other hand, a little nudging couldn't hurt.

"Thank you very much, sir," Cormac said as calmly as he knew how. He picked up his black leather jacket from over the back of the chair, walked out of the boxy little office, down the hall, and out of the building into the bright morning sunshine. He squinted into the blue sky.

He was free.

BACK AT his Jeep, he tossed the precious envelope on the passenger seat. After consideration, he picked it back up and tucked it in the inside pocket of his jacket. Like he expected it to disappear if he didn't have it with him.

"Shouldn't feel any different," he said out loud. "Not like anything's really changed."

Symbols are powerful, Amelia said. *You know that.*

This one meant he'd done it, crossed another bridge, taken another step toward normal. For certain values of normal. And now he had to figure out what to do with the rest of his life.

He made a call before even leaving the parking lot.

"It's done," he said when his cousin answered. "I'm off paper."

"Hallelujah," Ben O'Farrell sighed. "Congratulations."

"Congratulations to you for keeping me straight." Ben was also his lawyer.

"Group effort," Ben said. "Speaking of which, you have to come to New Moon tonight."

"Why?" he asked, wary.

"Kitty's planning a surprise party for you, to celebrate. I couldn't talk her out of it. Sorry."

Kitty, Ben's wife. Cormac had introduced them, years ago now. He still didn't know quite what to think about that. Smiled a little, though he wouldn't have if anyone had been watching. "She would want to do something like that, wouldn't she?"

"Yes, she would," Ben said, laughter and affection plain in his voice. "I thought you'd want some warning."

"Yeah, thanks. And Ben—thanks."

"You're welcome. You should call my mother next. She'll want to know."

"I will," he said, and hung up. His Aunt Ellen had been the one to take care of the Jeep while he was gone. Along with Ben and Kitty, she was his only family.

Cormac's manslaughter conviction had gotten him a slap on the wrist. There were so many other things he'd done that would have gotten him a longer sentence, a worse time of it if he'd been caught. If he'd gone down another road. The older he got—the longer he actually survived—the more grateful he was that Ben and his family had steered him away from that.

I'm grateful as well, Amelia said. *I'm not sure I would have liked you, if we'd met in your younger days.*

"I'm still surprised you like me now," he said. "You saying I'm not just a relationship of convenience?"

Hm, you're that, too. But still, I'm glad I met you when I did. She knew without him having to say it, that in his young wild days she might have tried to talk to him, but he sure as hell wouldn't have been able to listen. He would have been one of the ones she'd driven mad.

Amelia was one of those forks in the road that no one could have predicted.

SCREAMS, TERROR, the smell of death, a prison drenched in blood, fear sliding into a riot, unnatural and haunted. A monster, a shadowed thing with legs and arms but no visible face, with long claws and a wicked laugh. It had haunted those prison walls and would have killed him. It had already sliced open three men's throats, leaving their cell mates screaming in insanity and setting the whole prison at the edge of disaster.

Cormac had faced the demon down with nothing but his orange jumpsuit and bare hands. Then *she'd* been there, in his mind, guiding his hand. The spirit of a long-dead magician, a Victorian adventurer hanged for murder, who'd found a way to keep her soul alive—she said she could destroy the demon, but she needed his body, his living flesh and muscles, in order to do so. Finally, Cormac believed her. And not just because he didn't have a choice.

She had knowledge, but she needed him to fuel her spells. Her fire burned through him, tore the demon to pieces—

He woke up sometimes still expecting to see the washed-out ceiling of his prison cell, to feel the pressure of the bars on his back. He still shivered when he remembered that feeling, that something was lying in wait for him, waiting to rip open his throat, and he had no place to go.

Then he remembered her touch, the fire she brought with her.

He'd resisted her. He'd hated giving over part of himself, no matter what the reason. She hadn't been very happy about it either—she'd begun by trying to dominate him. Grab control and exert her will without having to argue with him. Slip on his body like a new suit. Of course, that wasn't an option.

They needed time to figure it out, but in the end they learned that they were stronger working together than they were apart. They could do more. They had a better chance for survival. And that was all either of them ever wanted.

HE BOTH did and didn't want to go to New Moon that night. He usually felt like that about the downtown restaurant that Ben and Kitty owned. The sense of obligation was . . . discomfiting. He didn't like feeling that he owed them, or anyone, something. Loyalty was difficult. It was an anchor holding him in place. At the same time, knowing he belonged here, with people who wanted to see him—that was a prize. A trophy for surviving, not just prison but his whole life so far. The number of times he probably shouldn't have made it, the number of guns he'd faced, the number of monsters—both human and supernatural—he'd sought out and mingled with hadn't given him great odds.

Yet here he was. The feeling of belonging was growing on him, like a pair of leather boots finally breaking in to mold to his feet.

The place was a few blocks south of Colfax, part of a collection of funky shops and restaurants that had sprung up around Broadway and the art museum in the last decade, an old brick block of a building that might have been a small-scale factory or warehouse sixty years ago, gone through refurbishment a couple of times over, and now had what reviewers called character.

He hesitated outside the restaurant's front door and took a deep breath.

He told himself not to flinch when the calls rang out. What did you shout at an ex-con newly off parole anyway? Happy freedom day? Happy not-on-parole-anymore? He was determined not to smirk at whatever banner she'd hung up. He wouldn't frown too hard at the proceedings. Depending on how earnest Kitty was about the whole thing, he might even smile.

You are making far too much of this.

Oh yeah? he thought. Just wait.

When he opened the door and entered the restaurant, nothing happened. In fact, everything looked normal. Everything sounded normal. Something jazzy played on the speakers, barely audible over the ambient noise of the crowd. The bar ran along one side of the interior, straight from the front door. Tables, about three-quarters occupied, filled the rest of the space. A pair of waitresses maneuvered among them on the hardwood floor, carrying trays, pitchers of beer. The ceiling was fashionably unfinished, painted ductwork and rafters giving the place an airy feel. The crowd was young to middle age, professional. The guy working the bar, Shaun, was the regular manager. He was always polite to Cormac, but usually glared at him with some suspicion. He knew Cormac's history. Cormac ignored him.

He walked in, and nothing changed. Nobody shouted surprise, nobody jumped out from behind anything. He stood a moment, wondering what was wrong.

Kitty approached from the bar, carrying a mug of some dark and dangerous-looking beer, which she offered him. Her smile crinkled, an expression of vast amusement.

"Congratulations," she said, and that was all.

Blinking, he took the beer, holding it at a slight distance as if he didn't know what to do with it.

"Surprised?" she said, lips parted in a grin that showed teeth. A challenging grin. Ben approached, coming up to look at him over her shoulder.

"You set me up," Cormac said to him.

"She set us both up. Not my fault." He held up his hands in a show of defense.

"You people don't have any faith in me at all, do you?" She heaved a dramatic sigh and turned to walk off to her usual table in back.

Kitty was cute. Not gorgeous, though she could probably approach it if she ever bothered with makeup and high heels and the whole getup. She chose comfort, in jeans and flat-heeled pumps and a short-sleeve blouse. About five-six, she had an athletic build and a quick grace about her. Her shoulder-length blond hair was loose, framing her face. Brown eyes. He'd known her for six or seven years now.

Ben he'd known his whole life, a fact that amazed him. Cormac sometimes had to adjust his own mental image of the man from the scruffy, gangly teenager he'd been when Cormac moved in with his family, to the focused, intense—and still kind of scruffy—adult he was now. He wore a blue button-up shirt untucked over khakis, hands shoved in his pockets. An average guy, likeable in spite of the law degree.

Side by side, the couple stalked to the back of the restaurant, retrieving their own beers from the bar. Cormac watched them, observing the undeniable, underlying truth of their lives: both Ben and Kitty were werewolves.

Cormac still flinched a little thinking of it. Werewolves were the bad guys, he'd known that truth since he was a boy learning to hunt from his father. His father didn't just hunt the usual game—he also took on vampires, werewolves, the supernatural creatures that most people thought were just stories, at least back then. Then, the inevitable happened. In hindsight, Cormac knew it was a matter of time. You hunted near-invulnerable monsters of the supernatural, ones that science and nature couldn't explain, that walked the Earth as proof that magic existed—eventually, you'd meet one you couldn't kill. And it would kill you. The men in the Bennett family who hunted all died young. He expected to die himself, by claw or fang, sooner rather than later. When Cormac was sixteen years old, a werewolf killed his father, and he hated them. Or thought he did. Then Kitty came along.

He'd meant to kill her. He'd been hired to kill her, a blatant attempt by his client to get her new and increasingly popular radio show off the air. Maybe he'd been stupid to take that job—the publicity of killing her on the air hadn't scared him, and he'd been confident, probably overconfident, of his ability to escape any repercussions after. He'd had a job, and his job was killing werewolves. She'd talked him out of it, live on the air, without breaking a sweat. At least not that he'd been able to see. They'd become something like friends.

When she'd needed a lawyer, he'd recommended

Ben. Later, he'd brought Ben along on a job—just backup was what he'd said, someone to call out if the bad guy came around from behind. But there'd been two bad guys, and one of them had gotten Ben. They'd made a pact as kids: if either of them was infected with lycanthropy, vampirism, or something worse, the other would kill him. When the moment came, Cormac couldn't do it. Couldn't kill the only person in the world he trusted, because Kitty proved that not all the werewolves were bad guys. Cormac took Ben to Kitty for help. Now they were married.

It seemed like a lifetime ago. Centuries ago. That all had happened to a different person, and now he came to the bar to drink with a couple of werewolves who were also his friends. His father would be so disappointed with him.

Stop minding your father, Amelia reprimanded him. *He's dead.*

"Yeah, well, so are you," he murmured.

As he watched Ben and Kitty, he could see their true nature in a dozen little ways that they weren't conscious of: the way their nostrils flared when the door opened and they smelled newcomers, the watchful look in their eyes, the stiffness in their shoulders when they got nervous. When they perched in their chairs, he could almost see ears pricking forward with interest. Kitty brushed along Ben as she sat, shoulder to shoulder, a gesture both animal and intimate. They kept watch over the bar, which they'd opened to be something of a den for their pack of wolves. Shaun was also a werewolf, and Cormac recognized a couple of others hanging out. Most people wouldn't see it, but Cormac knew what to look for.

When they were all seated with beers in hand, Ben raised his glass and said, "Cheers."

It was easy being comfortable here, drinking beer and sitting with friends. Being comfortable made him nervous.

"Does it feel different now?" Kitty asked.

He shrugged a little, the start of a deflection, but he changed his mind. "Yeah, it does. Feels like finally getting the keys to the handcuffs." He could feel the envelope resting in his inside pocket, pressing against his heart.

"Any big plans?" Ben asked.

"Vacation," Kitty said. "I'd go on vacation. Someplace with beaches. Or Disneyland! You could go to Disneyland."

Ben looked pained. "Your vacations don't tend to be all that relaxing."

"Someday," she answered. "*Someday,* I will have a vacation that doesn't go pear shaped."

Cormac's lip quirked in a smile. Kitty couldn't take a trip without combining it with work, which meant publicizing it, which meant attracting attention, and that was where the trouble started.

"Don't laugh," she muttered at him.

Ben said, "It's probably best not to make any life-changing decisions just yet. I've seen it happen—people go off paper, go crazy, throw themselves for a loop, fall into old habits, end up back in prison." Ben was a criminal defense attorney and spent a good chunk of his business escorting clients through the system.

"You don't trust me?" Cormac said.

"I'm your lawyer, it's my job to tell you these things."

Cormac picked at the edge of a coaster left on the table. "I'm thinking it's time I follow up the lead in Manitou Springs. Talk to Amy Scanlon's aunt." A different road, a new kind of job—he was ready to move on. Maybe this really was what he ought to be doing with the rest of his life.

"You okay with that?" Kitty asked. "You want company? Me being there might make things a little easier." She was a born diplomat, and for some reason she didn't think Cormac, in his leather jacket and biker boots, approaching some grief-stricken old lady, was a particularly good idea. Go figure.

"No, I'll be fine. I'm just getting fidgety. The part of Scanlon's book we put online might give us something eventually, but I don't think we can wait much longer."

Ben turned to Kitty. "You still don't have anything from Grant? Tina?"

"They're checking in. You know how this stuff works, it's hit or miss. More misses than hits, usually. It's not a science."

Kitty had a whole collection of contacts, real-deal mediums, magicians, and ghost hunters in addition to the vampires and lycanthropes she knew. She'd met most of them through her radio show. Each of them provided various bits and pieces of information, but they still didn't have the whole picture—the key to decoding Scanlon's book, which in turn might be the key to solving an even bigger problem: the vampire Roman.

"Maybe this one'll be a hit," Cormac said.

Even though it meant telling this woman that her long-lost niece was dead. And it meant going back to the end of Amelia's life.

Amelia turned unusually quiet whenever the subject of Manitou Springs came up. They'd both been avoiding it. With his parole over, Cormac was running out of excuses to put off the trip.

He kept himself to one beer and didn't talk much, but that was usual. Watched Ben and Kitty and their easy way of bantering. They had some friends come through—and not just members of their werewolf pack. Normal people, coworkers and contacts, who chatted and laughed with them. Talked about ordinary things. Ben and Kitty, they had a life. They may have been werewolves, but this wasn't the first time Cormac felt like the outcast next to them.

Before he started getting too uncomfortable, Cormac bowed himself out. They only argued a little for show, and Cormac assured them that he was fine, he just needed some rest. The usual song and dance. The normality of a life he wasn't sure he'd ever really get used to.

Chapter 2

AFTER GETTING out of prison, Cormac had moved into a rundown studio apartment off the Boulder Turnpike on the northwest side of Denver. Wasn't much, but he didn't need much. A place to sleep, a lock to keep out bad guys. It wasn't like he had people over much. Or at all.

For a while he'd had a part-time job restocking at a warehouse, mostly to keep Porter happy and give the impression of being an upstanding citizen. He'd had to take time off when he broke his arm a few months ago, and he was long since past the time when he should think about going back. He didn't need much money, but he needed some. His pre-prison savings wouldn't last forever. He'd earned a surprising amount of cash doing some freelance detective work for Kitty and Ben, and for the Denver Police Department. The idea of going full time—essentially becoming a supernatural private investigator—had seemed ridiculous.

But he was on the verge of thinking that maybe there really was a demand for this kind of thing, and maybe he really could make a living at it. It was just another kind of hunting, after all. He wasn't exactly cut out for working for someone else.

Back home, very late at night now but he didn't tend to sleep much anyway, he fired up his laptop. The machine was another gift from Ben, a "welcome home" after prison. Cormac had never had a computer in his life, had never needed one. Well, now he did, he guessed.

Amelia had insisted on putting magical protections on the laptop, a protective rune here and an arcane mark there. Cormac wasn't sure electronics worked that way, that *magic* worked that way. *It couldn't hurt,* Amelia had said. But it could, if it screwed up the computer's inner workings.

We had electricity even in my day, Amelia had said grumpily. *It's all wires and power in the end. Making connections and letting in or keeping out energies that might be dangerous. Trust me.*

His e-mail account had been strangely free of spam since he set it up.

The current problem: Amy Scanlon's book of shadows. Amy Scanlon had been a possibly-not-entirely-sane—she believed herself to be a modern-day avatar of Zoroaster—but immensely talented magician.

Kitty had inherited her book of shadows, her magician's diary, stored on a USB drive. Kitty was sure the thing was packed with all kinds of information about Dux Bellorum and the Long Game. *That* was the real mystery Kitty was trying to solve: Dux Bellorum—Roman, Gaius Albinus, Mr. White, who knew what other names he went by—was a two-thousand-year-old vampire, and he had a plan, which seemed to be nearing its climax. Dux Bellorum—the leader of war. Cormac didn't often get nervous, but this guy made him nervous. He'd faced him down exactly once, and Roman had clearly been using his long existence to become as adept as inhumanly possible at waging supernatural war. He had a plan to take over the world: the Long Game. Trouble was, nobody knew just how he was going to do it. He was gathering allies, bringing other vampire Masters around the world under his influence. Building an army, with him as its general. Somehow, Kitty had managed to put herself at the head of those trying to oppose him. Cormac had her back.

Now Kitty had this book that promised to offer answers to all the riddles, just like that. Too bad the whole thing was in code.

Since they didn't know how to break the book's code, they decided to crowdsource it. Put it up online and see what happened. Worst case scenario, someone would break the code and find enough magical secrets to take over the world. Kitty thought the risk was worth it. Cormac had taken on the responsibility of keeping track of the e-mails associated with the Web site. The first three or four weeks, nothing happened.

But then serious messages started coming in. Only a few at first. Now, they arrived a dozen or so a week. A couple of online forums had picked up on the book of shadows, posted links, and started discussions. Cormac followed those as well. Most of the discussions assumed the book was old, some Renaissance alchemist's journal that had been scanned, digitized, and posted by an amateur scholar. Kitty hadn't posted any identifying information about the author—she'd become protective of Amy Scanlon's private life. These dabblers treated the book and its code as an interesting problem and nothing more.

Five e-mails this evening. Usually, they came from borderline nutjobs begging for the secret of the universe or declaring that they *had* the secret of the universe, and they wanted to meet in person or send their own five-thousand-page book of shadows. Today, one of them was different.

"Hi. Whoever this is. I don't know the code, but I know the diagrams, some of the formulas—this looks like Amy Scanlon's book. I was in her coven in Taos,

New Mexico, about six years ago. She started traveling, but I haven't heard from her in a couple of years. Do you know where she is?" The e-mail listed a name and phone number. A trusting person, to hand out that information.

Cormac didn't know how to tell her that Scanlon was dead, killed at the center of a mystery they desperately needed to solve. He couldn't imagine trying to explain it and be sympathetic at the same time. He forwarded the message to Kitty to let her answer it. She was the diplomat and camp counselor. He stuck to lurking on forums and searching for articles that might give him more pieces. Clues to the mystery they'd set themselves to solving.

I quite like the idea of supernatural investigation. We could be the magical Sherlock Holmes and Watson.

"Yeah, but which of us is which?"

Well, I think that's rather obvious, don't you?

He snorted.

Hunting for information wasn't too far off from hunting game, in the end. You had to have a good idea of what you were looking for and the places you'd be most likely to find it. Keep an open mind and your vision wide—focus too hard on one thing, you miss stray movement at the edges of your perception. Most of all, you had to be patient.

When it came to Scanlon's grimoire, though, he was losing patience.

"It's time to go to Manitou," he said.

Silence from Amelia.

Part of the book of shadows—the part Kitty kept offline—was biographical, uncoded, and mentioned one of Scanlon's mentors, an aunt living an hour or so down the freeway from Denver.

"We've got no other leads."

Still nothing. He sighed, wondering at the weird twists in his life that brought him to standing in his apartment, talking to himself.

"You want to talk about this in person?" he said.

After a moment she answered, *If you like.*

What the hell, it was probably time for bed anyway.

BACK IN prison, Cormac spent much of his time thinking about a meadow.

The place was a memory of a high mountain valley in Grand County where his father used to take him hunting. Mundane hunting for elk and deer with licenses and rifles and standard, non-silver bullets. Douglas Bennett's main line of work had been as a guide on high-end outfitting trips, leading hunting parties into the backwoods of the Rockies to bag trophies. Sometimes when they were on their own, just him and his father, they'd camp in this meadow, a stretch filled with thick grasses, surrounded by lodgepole pines and a rushing stream cutting through the middle. Boil coffee on a butane camp stove before dawn, watch the sunrise as mist burned off the creek. Nothing smelled as clean as those mornings.

To keep himself from going entirely crazy in his ten-by-ten cell, he imagined himself back there. He'd lay on his metal cot and thin mattress and fall asleep by putting himself somewhere else. Over time, the place grew in detail, richness. He could see individual blades of grass blowing in a faint breeze, hear water rushing over rocks in the creek. Feel the sun on his face as he tipped his head back, watching white clouds scudding across an impossibly blue sky.

Habit kept bringing him back. Also, in a sense, this was where he'd met Amelia. This was how she'd found her way into his mind. This was where they talked.

In waking hours, she was a disembodied voice, a presence watching the world over his shoulder. When he closed his eyes, opened his mind, put himself in the place where he'd always felt most at home—safest—he saw her. She found him.

There was a boulder, a weathered outcrop of granite where he sat to watch the meadow and its valley. This was where she joined him. At first, back in prison, she'd approach cautiously and stand a few yards off, regarding him skeptically as if negotiating with a hired laborer.

Now, after all they'd been through, she sat in the

grass nearby, legs folded to the side, her long skirt spread around her, and gazed out at the scene with him. Her clothing was antique, formal—dark gray skirt, white shirt with a high collar and touch of lace at the sleeves. Her black hair was wrapped in a tight bun, pinned to the back of her head, and she wore a flat, feathered hat. She was, would always be, a woman in her mid-twenties, straight and severe in demeanor, frowning as she studied the world with dark eyes.

She took a deep breath, sighed in satisfaction, and he had to remind himself that she wasn't exactly alive. Here, she spoke, more than just a voice. She had expression, gestures, shrugs and frowns. She was almost real.

"We're going, you know. We have to go," he said.

"I know." She didn't seem agitated or upset about it, here. She sat calmly, gazing out.

"You ready for this?" he asked.

"Why wouldn't I be?" She wouldn't look at him. Why would she, with a view like this? The world was in winter, but the meadow here was bright, warm summer.

"Manitou is where it happened. Where that girl was murdered, where they arrested you."

"I don't remember discussing this with you."

Memories bled between them in both directions. She knew why this valley was so important, she knew what had happened to his father. And he knew what had happened to her. "It was in that old newspaper story."

Her voice went soft. "Ah yes. Of course."

"So. Are you ready?"

She didn't answer right away, not even in a righteous huff to disguise whatever she actually felt. Ultimately, what she felt didn't matter—he had the body, he needed to go to Manitou Springs despite her bad memories of the place, so he'd go. But she could make things difficult if she wanted to, so he had to look her in the eyes, to ask.

"I'll be fine," she said finally, with determination, glancing at him over her shoulder. "It happened a hundred years ago. More than a hundred years ago. It's done with." She had drawn her knees up and sat hugging them to her chest, a strangely childlike gesture.

They'd find out soon enough how she really felt.

WHEN AMELIA was a little girl, she had wanted to see fairies so very badly. She spent hours, days, in a glen by a fishpond on the family's estate, outside the village of Sevenoaks, setting out bread crumbs and bowls of milk, hanging colored ribbons and silver bells, anything that might entice the creatures from their leafy bowers where she imagined them hiding, shy and fearful. The perch in the pond and finches in the undergrowth got most of the bread crumbs, and the only creatures she ever saw hiding there were several generations of a family of mice, living and breeding in their dens under the tree roots. But there'd been magic in that place, she'd felt it, a spark bubbling up from the spring that fed the pond, an otherworldliness in the green of the moss covering the stones. She'd started reading about Grail lore then, wondering if her pond was the Chalice Well, or perhaps *a* chalice well, and that had led her to the whole Arthurian mythos, far beyond the Tennyson she got from her governess, and she learned about the spirit of the land and ley lines. She'd found out about the Uffington White Horse carved out of a hillside in Oxfordshire and begged her parents for an outing there, which they accomplished when she was sixteen. She speculated wildly about its origins, its no-doubt magical purpose, and what great ritual or spell had been wrought on the location. Predictably, her parents and brother suggested she ought to direct her attention and energies toward more ladylike pursuits, most importantly her inevitable marriage. Her childish interest in magic and fairies and the wights living in old Celtic hill forts might have been amusing when she was a girl in braids and pinafores. But she would soon be a lady, they said. That was the beginning of all the mess that followed.

She read every moment she could, books that her tutors would never have approved, clandestine pamphlets and penny dreadfuls about the Golden Dawn and Freemasonry and alchemical lore. Most of it was bunk, but she picked out the threads that felt true. When she was eighteen, she worked her first real spell, a simple charm to make a length of thread impossible to cut. It worked. So did the spell to uncharm the thread. She felt powerful. With such magic she could bind the world.

That was when she decided she would not marry, because she could not imagine any husband in the world allowing his wife to study and work magic, and she could not imagine keeping such a thing secret from the person she was meant to spend her life with. Never mind how she would hide such a thing from children. She was not interested in children. Therefore, no marriage for her. Of course, this was the precise moment that Arthur Pembroke appeared to court her. She could still see him standing in her father's parlor, gaping in astonishment that she had just told him no.

Objectively, she could observe that he was considered a very good catch at the time. In hindsight, especially considering what happened to her just a few years later, she could admit that her life with him most likely would not have been horrible. She'd looked for him, when Cormac got out of prison and had access to the resources. Pembroke had found a different girl to marry, had continued on in his family's textile export business. Then he'd got a commission and commanded a regiment in World War I. He'd been killed at the Somme. She'd have been widowed at forty, undoubtedly with children to care for, in a precarious financial situation as the war had disrupted trade. Just as his wife had been. It all seemed very sad to Amelia.

She had missed so much, cloistered with no body and little awareness for that hundred years. It might have all gone differently, if she'd actually seen fairies in the long-ago glen. If she had, she might have stopped looking for magic.

She had been born a hundred years too early. Her soul should have been patient, so she could be born into a world where she could choose not to marry, not to have children, and no one would think it strange. She would not have been so outcast.

Now, she was simply out of place, out of step, bodiless, and with a broken soul that lived only because Cormac had not yet learned how to eject her entirely. He would grow strong enough to do so, someday. He would grow tired of playing host. With the magic they practiced, she was teaching him the means by which he could dispel her, if he chose. Then she would truly die.

She *still* wasn't ready to die. All this time, all this strangeness, she still wanted to live. She must make herself useful to Cormac. She must make herself necessary, so that he would not think of rejecting her. Cormac, the man who prided himself on his loneliness. He didn't need anyone.

Chapter 3

CORMAC ARRIVED in Manitou Springs at midday. After parking the Jeep on a side street, he walked to Soda Springs Park, a sheltered stretch of space along the creek in the middle of town. The bare winter branches and trunks of a row of trees and shrubbery gave a semblance of seclusion from the nearby road. Some modern hippie types with white-kid dreads and creative piercings gathered under a covered picnic area and gave him a passing glance.

I don't remember any of this, Amelia said. *Heavens, when did this all become so built over? The streets, the trees—it all seems wrong. We can't possibly be in the right town, but I know we are, because I remember that view of the mountains, and that row of houses there. But wasn't there a gazebo here, and not that ugly thing?*

She meant the picnic shelter, clearly a product of modern parks-and-rec department utility. Her chatter was nervous. Amelia was tough. Ruthless, when it came to her own survival—after all, she'd managed to at least partly survive her own hanging and find a way to continue on, whatever the form. But Cormac could feel the trepidation she'd suppressed for over a century, now boiling up. He got ready to power through it.

A quick search online revealed that Amy Scanlon's aunt, Judi Scanlon, ran a "supernatural" walking tour of Manitou Springs. Not just a ghost tour, but a tour that promised to highlight all of the town's supernatural points of interest, from Native American sacred sites to the so-called magic surrounding its famous springs, and so on. Cormac signed them up as a way to gauge the woman before formally meeting her, rather than just walking up to her to tell her that her niece was dead, and could she please help decode the book.

Even in winter a good collection of tourists gathered for the tour, which met at the paved space at the park entrance. The relatively warm, sunny day had brought them out, in ski vests and hip knitted hats. A solitary guy in his leather jacket and sunglasses, Cormac looked out of place. He kept to the edges of the group and watched.

When a lone, older woman came up the sidewalk, wrapped in a colorful wool coat and striding like she was on a mission, Cormac guessed this was Judi

Scanlon. Surveying the group, she offered a broad smile, rubbing her hands together, like she was scheming. "You all here for the tour? Great! I'm Judi, thanks for coming out on this chilly day. Let's get started, all right?"

Cormac worried that she might be into icebreakers—demanding to know everyone's names and where they were from. But she didn't go there, just marched on, leading the group to the sidewalk. Judi was vibrant, one of those types who always seemed to be volunteering at libraries or walking in charity fundraisers. Stout without being fat, with short silver hair under a baseball cap, an oversized comfortable sweater and sensible sneakers.

We're going to have to tell this kindly woman what happened to her niece, Amelia said.

Cormac still hadn't figured out exactly how that was going to happen. He was playing this by ear. He trailed along at the end of the group, arms crossed, listening to history he mostly already knew.

Tucked in at the base of Pikes Peak, Manitou Springs had been a tourist town for some hundred and thirty years. Its collection of mineral springs made it an early destination for rich health nuts and tuberculosis patients who'd traveled west in the late eighteen hundreds to take advantage of the dry climate. The wealthy founders of nearby Colorado Springs had vacation homes here. A collection of gingerbread

Victorian mansions remained, but most of the businesses on the main drag had been converted to T-shirt shops, art galleries, and trendy restaurants.

Manitou was a storied city, starting out on the frontier of the Old West, with prospectors and explorers, even a few gunslingers and gamblers, along with the original Mexican settlers and Native Americans getting pushed out by the brand new world. Lots of travelers, which meant lots of history, lots of lore, lots of ghost stories. Judi seemed to know them all.

Amelia knew a number of them herself—some of these ghosts had been haunting buildings in the town for a long time. She murmured corrections to Judi's commentary in the back of Cormac's mind and added her own observations about what buildings had been there back in the day, which hadn't, what had changed, and what no longer existed. Like any traveler coming back to any spot after a long absence, some of it was familiar, some of it utterly changed. Ten years, a hundred years, didn't seem to make a difference.

The word "Manitou" comes from the Algonquin tribe of Indians, she murmured. Cormac thought she might have been talking to herself, repeating old lore. *It refers to a kind of nature spirit, as I understand it, although I've read some authors who insist that* manitou *refers to gods. There was so much argument, a hundred years ago, about whether the Indians even had gods. Mostly among missionaries, I imagine.*

Does anyone still argue about such things? I should do some reading on it. At any rate, I'm certain the word has nothing at all to do with local legends or native spirits. I've even heard tell someone got the name from Longfellow, as if that was the only relevant lore any of them had encountered—unacademic drivel, hardly worth speaking of. Really, the Algonquin are an eastern tribe and have nothing to do with this part of the country.

She was distracting herself from more concrete memories, he realized.

The tour progressed to a certain street, and Amelia grew quieter, until she stopped talking at all.

"Next I'm going to tell you what's probably the most gruesome story on this tour—don't say I didn't warn you," Judi said, with a wink and a grin, and approached one of the gingerbread Victorians at the end of the block. It was two stories tall with dormer windows in the attic, and a porch wrapped around two sides of the house, all of it painted blue with white trim, hooks over the porch where planters would hang in summer, brass light fixture by the door, the works.

Judi drew a key from a pocket and gestured them up. "I have permission from the owner to bring you inside, if you'll step up this way."

Cormac stopped at the foot of the porch's stairs.

I know this house, Amelia whispered. *It's different—*

it stood alone, then. The street's been built up. I would have walked right past it. But I know it. . . .

Judi began her lecture. "In 1900, this house witnessed a terrible murder. A beautiful young woman, Lydia Harcourt, beloved by the whole town, met her end here, murdered in what can only be described as a demonic ritual by the most unlikely perpetrator imaginable—an English noblewoman. Let's go inside."

Gathered on the porch, the rest of the tour-goers murmured with interest. Cormac tried to take a step—and couldn't move. A freezing dread had traveled down his legs, and Amelia's presence overwhelmed him.

I remember. I can smell the blood.

Her memory gave him the scent of it, like the smell of a butcher shop, tangy and foreboding.

That was over a hundred years ago, he thought at her. Let's go in.

Their partnership worked because he kept possession of his body. Unless they were explaining or working magic—and often, even then, when Amelia fed him instructions rather than performing the movements herself—Cormac was in control. Her fear had overridden his control. She wasn't going to let him move.

An anger grew up in him, his thoughts turning hard: Do they say "Get back on the horse" where you're from? Just let me go in and get it over with.

The rest of the tour was already in the house, and Judi waited at the front door, looking out. "Is everything all right? I promise, it isn't too scary for a big tough guy like you." She wore an amused smile.

Gritting his teeth, Cormac made an angry shove at himself, and his legs moved. They scuffed on the walkway, but they moved.

Judi described the day in 1900 when the door burst open and people saw the bloody corpse of Lydia Harcourt lying on the floor, and Lady Amelia Parker bending over her, kneeling in a pool of blood, perpetrating some ungodly ritual on the body. A circle had been drawn on the floor in chalk, incense burned, lit candles flared, the whole nine yards. Like something out of a horror movie with all the usual clichés.

The house had been restored since then, and the story clashed with the Victorian parlor setting: clean hardwood floor, a rug at the base of a staircase, padded straight-backed chairs, a mirror and table against one wall, nondescript paintings of flowers hanging at intervals. It looked like a dozen other restored houses in town. But Judi painted a picture, and Amelia's memories rose up.

It was such a horrible crime, she murmured, recovering, her explorer's mind returning. *This all looks so . . . polite, compared to when I last saw this place.*

Through her, he saw that scene. It was more than déjà vu, this feeling Amelia's perspective gave him.

He had two memories in one body, and her memories of this place were strong, filled with emotion—regret, anger, despair.

Her perspective shifted the setting, overlaying what had happened with how the room looked now, and the double vision gave him vertigo. He almost put his hand out to steady himself. There was the body of the girl Amelia had been accused of murdering, her throat cut deeply, her head bent back unnaturally; there was the pool of blood around her; there were the candles and mirror of the spell Amelia worked to try to question the victim from beyond the grave. That was how the locals had found her, bent over the bloody scene, a witch out of a nightmare.

"This is where the body lay when the local constabulary burst through the door," the guide said, pointing to the side of the room near the staircase. "There was a struggle as the murderer threw her tools at them and made to flee out the back door, but she wasn't fast enough. She didn't escape."

Amelia was looking at a different spot. The memories played out.

"No," Cormac said. He pointed to an area four feet over, more in the center of the room than to the side. "The body was there. They came in—Amelia had to turn to see them. She didn't struggle. She knew what it looked like, knew they weren't going to listen to anything she had to say to defend herself." His voice faded; he wasn't sure if he'd been passing along her words, or if he was trying to explain the emotions she was showing him.

The other half dozen people on the tour stared. Rather than apologize or try to explain what he knew, he frowned back and stayed quiet.

Judi studied him while picking up her spiel and carrying on. "The horror of it ensured the crime would make all the newspapers. . . ."

If Amelia had a body, she might have been holding a breath that she now released. The memory faded, along with the scent of blood, and the reality of the present won out. This was a competently restored house, a moderately accurate historical tour, and the emotional hooks that dug into their skin eased away.

Judi had still more story to tell: "As you might imagine, many stories about this house have grown up over the years. Screams on certain nights, pools of blood appearing at midnight. Many people are convinced that poor Lydia's ghost haunts the place where she was killed. Some people say that Amelia Parker's ghost also lingers here, still stalking her victim after death. . . ."

Well, we know that's *wrong,* Amelia thought with a huff.

I don't know—you're here, aren't you? Maybe we should knock over a chair, just for fun.

She was indignant. *I don't think so.*

Finally, they left the house.

You all right? Cormac asked that corner of his mind.

I—yes. I think I am. It's better, now that I've seen it. I needed to see it. You were right.

I'm sorry, he thought stiffly, unaccustomed to the sentiment. It was stupid luck that they caught you.

I'm not one to say that all things happen for a reason. But, well, here I am. I'm not inclined to argue. Let's move on.

The guide led them down the street, the circular tour curving back to the park where they'd started, and she shared a couple more stories of lurid suicides and Native American magic. Cormac started to think about how he was going to approach Judi. The tour she led was full of supernatural weirdness, but how much of it was just stories for her? How much did she really believe? Amy Scanlon had listed her as a mentor—how much did the woman really know about magic?

The tour ended back at the park. The tourists drifted off, but Judi lingered, like he thought she might, regarding Cormac with curiosity. He waited for her to ask the questions she so obviously had.

"Did you enjoy the tour?" she asked.

He smirked, amused at the roundabout lead-in. "I did. Thanks." Another beat of waiting.

"You're very interested in the Harcourt murder, I

take it," she said finally, leading to the real question. "Why?"

He nodded, acknowledging. "I'm interested in Amelia Parker. She didn't kill the girl. She was innocent."

"Then who did kill her?"

There wasn't a subtle way to say it. "The demon Amelia was hunting."

The tour guide's eyes narrowed. "You know what? I've always thought it was something like that. What makes you think so?"

"I've talked to Amelia," Cormac said, just to see the reaction.

Her eyes widened in wonder. Not skepticism, which would have prompted a shutting down of expression, not an opening up, like this. He kept his expression still.

After a moment she said, "Would you like to come back to my shop for some tea?"

He said yes.

Chapter 4

TURNED OUT, Judi and her partner owned a gift shop on Canon Avenue, just off the highway, part of a row of restored nineteenth-century storefronts. The MANITOU WISHING WELL, according to the sign. The tour guiding was a sideline; Judi was interested in the history and liked to tell stories.

"Frida really knows more about things like talking to ghosts," she said. "When it comes to the more esoteric topics like that, I'm really only a dabbler."

The way her niece talked about her, Cormac doubted that. Thoughts? he asked Amelia.

I'm reserving judgment.

A soft bell rang when she opened the door, and Judi led him inside. The shop was exactly what he expected: racks of T-shirts, sweatshirts, mugs, knickknacks; shelves full of ceramic hummingbirds, so-called collectibles; bags of Rocky Mountain–themed candy, neo-antiques, and the like. The place had a vibe to it, though. The further back they went into the shop, the deeper into that world, the less fake and commercial it seemed, until they reached the shelves of crystals, books on ley lines, and weird tarot cards.

There's magic here, Amelia said. *I can see some of the signs, charms on the wall there and there. Protection. But also encouraging generosity. Interesting.*

"Frida, I've brought company," Judi called.

A woman appeared through a doorway behind the counter running along the side of the store. She had Native American heritage: long, straight black hair streaked with some gray hanging loose down her back, sandstone-brown skin, dark eyes. Shorter than Judi, she was round, matronly, and wore a blue tunic shirt with jeans. Like Judi, she wasn't in her prime—maybe midsixties—but still gave off an air of energy and determination.

"Who is it?"

Judi presented him, and he resisted an urge to shove his hands in his pockets and duck his head sheepishly. "My name's Cormac Bennett."

"He took the tour, and he says he's spoken to Amelia Parker, the Lydia Harcourt murderer," Judi said. "I thought it might be nicer if we could all sit together over tea. Or coffee, Mr. Bennett?"

Tea, Amelia proposed, predictably. "Tea's fine."

Frida didn't bother being at all circumspect when she said to Judi, "Do you know he has two auras?"

"No, but I can't say I'm surprised," Judi said. "Let me go plug the kettle in." She skirted around the counter to the back room while Frida studied him. Cormac ignored her, absently looking at stained glass butterfly ornaments hanging from a rack without really seeing them. Eventually, she followed Judi to the back, and they had a hushed conversation.

They're suspicious.

Of course they are, he thought. He didn't even blame them. He was a surly-looking guy who'd spent his whole life working on being intimidating. Hadn't been a handicap until now.

Perhaps we should have invited Kitty along after all.

Well, too late now. They'd have to make this work somehow.

A faint patter sounded, then a thud as a cat jumped from behind the counter to the glass surface. It should have slid, but the animal braced, stopped, and elegantly arranged itself to a sitting position, looking like an Egyptian statue. The animal was hairless, probably bred that way, but that didn't make it any less bizarre, with huge ears, knobby feet, and velvety wrinkly skin. The tail wrapped around its legs was a skinny stick. It had big green eyes and an accusing stare. Even the cat was suspicious.

Good God, what's wrong with it? Amelia exclaimed.

It's supposed to be that way, I think. He held his

hand out to the creature. The cat's nose wrinkled, but it didn't offer to sniff, much less approach for petting. Just kept that glare focused on him.

"Esther is generally a good judge of character," Judi said, emerging from the back room holding two mugs.

"That so?" He accepted one of the mugs.

"She sees it—you have two auras." Frida said it as an accusation as she reappeared with a mug of her own.

"So I've been told." Cormac sipped. It was a green tea with something else mixed in.

Ginger, Amelia offered. *Lovely.* Amelia appreciated the tea more than he did; since he didn't really have an opinion about tea one way or another, he drank it. At least it was in a solid mug and not some dainty china cup.

"The two auras thing doesn't surprise you?" Judi said. A prompt.

He was happy enough not having to mention Amy Scanlon right away. "No, not really. So what exactly does two auras look like?"

Frida pursed her lips, considered. Cormac tensed under the scrutiny, but held his ground. Sipped tea calmly. "It's double vision, like you're out of focus. Though I'm thinking part of that is just you, yeah? But there's one strong layer, then another layer under that. A lot of red, a lot of blue, and they're not merged at all like they should be—two auras instead of one with many colors. And it's clouded, like you're not too sure about things. Can't say I've ever seen anything like it. You have an explanation?"

They must have had some idea of what he was going to say, the expectant way they were looking at him. "It's Amelia Parker," he said. "We met. She, ah, needed a ride. And here we are."

The two women blinked back at him, speechless.

Rather blunt. You might have frightened even them.

His mustache crinkled in a wry smile, and he spread his hands as if to say, just so.

"I . . . see," Judi said, nodding. "That's how you know so much about the murder, then."

The cat swished its naked tail and stalked along the counter to Frida's waiting hand, arching her back as the woman stroked her.

He set the mug on the counter. "I'm not really here about the Harcourt murder or Amelia Parker," he said. "Let me be straight with you. I've come to talk about Amy Scanlon."

The silver-haired woman blanched and leaned against Frida. Brow creased with concern, Frida steadied her.

"She's dead, isn't she?" Judi said, and Cormac didn't deny it. "We felt it, but we couldn't guess how, or why. About a month ago, right? Late at night, I started sweating and shaking and couldn't stop."

"I'm sorry," Cormac said.

"What happened? How? Did you know her, you must have known her. . . ."

"Hon, do you need to sit down?" Frida asked, both hands on Judi now.

"No, no, it's all right," she said, patting Frida's arm. "What on Earth am I going to tell her parents? I kept telling them she'd come home when she was ready. She's an explorer, nothing they could do or say would stop that, but I made them believe she'd come home some day."

"You know what she was, then?" he asked. "You know what she was into?"

"I . . . I'm the one who initiated her."

Cormac drew a set of folded sheets of paper from his jacket pocket. "Then maybe you can interpret this."

He watched their reaction to the printed sheets from Amy's book of shadows. Judi raised the pages, her gaze narrowed with interest. Frida—she took a step back, as if she didn't want even a stray look at them.

He said, "A friend of mine, I guess you could say she inherited the book of shadows. We've been trying to break the code. Amy mentioned you in her diary. We thought maybe you could help."

Frida glared at him. "Would you excuse us a moment?" She took hold of Judi's arm and pulled her to the back room for another hushed conference. The cat looked after them, then licked its paw with great concentration.

Cormac listened closely, but they conducted their argument in whispers and he couldn't make out what they said. Probably discussing whether this might be some kind of scam and if they could trust him. He wondered what his aura—auras—said about that.

But the question is—should they trust us? Honestly?

The two women emerged, Frida glowering and suspicious, Judi looking thoughtful. Side by side, they stood on one side of the counter and regarded him, as if he were a customer asking about T-shirt sizes.

"Mr. Bennett—you have all of Amy's book of shadows, don't you? The whole thing?"

"Yeah. I can get you a copy, if you can help with the code." He didn't mention that most of it was already online. Let them figure it out.

They looked at each other, a silent conversation between old friends, and he guessed they wanted more from him than the book.

"I have a question, Mr. Bennett. Why? I know—knew—Amy, and maybe I didn't know exactly what she was working on, but I have some idea what she was capable of. Why do you want access to that? Why should I help give you access to that? Assuming I can." She stood resolute, though her eyes were pink, on the edge of shedding tears.

He looked away, chuckled. "That's a really long story." He should have known just asking them wouldn't work—he looked like a hit man.

"It's Amelia Parker, isn't it?" said the ever-suspicious Frida. "She was a wizard then, and she still is. So what's she need Amy's book for?"

Tell them it isn't for me, it isn't for us. Tell them the fate of the world—

They'd never believe that, he thought back. However true it might be. . . . The whole story really was long and unbelievable—even more unbelievable than him carrying around Amelia. Kitty could get away with just asking, and would be able to think up an explanation that sounded important without sounding outlandish. He gave it a try.

"Amy got mixed up with some very dangerous people," he said simply. "I need to find out what she knew about them, so that no one else gets hurt." There, that sounded good. Didn't it? In the back of his head, Amelia was watchful.

That seemed to put Judi at her ease. Frida, not so much, but Judi was the one who gave the decisive nod. "I think I can decode this for you, Mr. Bennett. But I need something from you first."

"That's fair."

"You're obviously experienced in the arcane. You certainly seem to have a unique perspective on things—Amelia Parker is here now, isn't she? She's listening to all of this?"

"That's right," he said.

"Then you might be just the person we need for this."

Out with it, Amelia grumbled.

Settle down, Cormac thought.

It was Frida who said, "I think we need your help."

He didn't show the surprise he felt. What could these two biddies possibly need his help for?

Judi said, "Let me tell you a story, Mr. Bennett. . . ."

"IN 1895, a man named Milo Kuzniak came into Manitou claiming to have found gold in the hills west of town. No one believed him—people had been looking for gold in the area for going on fifty years, any gold to be had was already found. The rush was over. He persisted, filed claims, bought equipment, camped in the hills, ran off passersby with a shotgun, and bragged in town about what he would find. Generally made a nuisance of himself."

They'd retreated to seats in the back of the store. Customers came in at one point, and Frida helped them when they bought some candy. She came back with a teapot and refilled their tea.

"Then some strange things started happening. Horses shied away from his claim. A photographer hiking with his equipment in the area fell and broke his leg, and the men and burro sent to carry him back to town became hopelessly lost. Moans and screams were heard from the land late at night, but no one ever saw mischief afoot. Those who went to investigate didn't find anything, but they felt a powerful dread the further into Milo's claim they went. A point came when most men refused to go there at all.

"Milo started telling wild tales, that he'd found a book of spells and was now a powerful magician, that he'd summoned ghosts to do his bidding and guard his territory. He had otherworldly traps and torments designed to repel intruders. This must have been intriguing as well as frightening, but no one had any way of proving it. The stories grew more sinister as time went on. The people of Manitou loved nothing more than a good scary story, and this was a whopper."

You ever hear about this guy? Cormac questioned Amelia.

No, I never did.

Judi continued. "Then local gentleman Augustus Crane decided to do something about Kuzniak and his tall tales. He was a great believer in magic, held séances in his house, was well known in Spiritualist circles. The town held him in high esteem, because he brought such a scientific gravity to his proceedings. One could not help but take him seriously. It was, he decided, up to him to stop this magical menace before he did real harm. The area wasn't big enough for two self-proclaimed magicians. He studied his books, asked advice of the great Spiritualists of his day, organized the spell he would use to put Milo Kuzniak in his place. Then he went to Kuzniak's claim, where the man had camped out."

I have heard of Augustus Crane, Amelia said. *People were still mourning him when I arrived in town.*

"They had what might be called a wizards' duel, a showdown at midnight under a full moon. Some of the folk from town, other members of Crane's Spiritualist circle, came with him to witness. None of them could say exactly what happened. Crane challenged Kuzniak. Kuzniak refused to give way. So Crane cast a spell that was designed to weaken Kuzniak, remove his magic—remove his will to antagonize the town. Crane believed the spell would weaken him to the point of sickness and drive Milo back to wherever he'd come from. But that didn't happen. None of that happened."

The flair for storytelling Judi had brought to the walking tour came through here. "Milo stood unflinching before him—at a loss, observers said. Not even bothering to work a magical defense. But this was a ruse. Milo had made preparations before Augustus arrived, and he was very well defended when

Augustus cast his spell. As soon as he did, Milo's defenses came to the fore, and rather than defeating his opponent, Crane himself was struck dead where he stood. Some claimed they saw a bolt of lightning strike him from the clear sky. Some say the burst of electricity traveled up from the ground and electrocuted him. Others say the power came from Milo Kuzniak's eyes, or his outstretched hands. Whatever it was, Augustus Crane ended up flat on the ground, dead."

"You left this story off the walking tour," Cormac said.

Judi ignored him and made the mystery at the heart of her story plain. "To this day, no one knows what killed him, only that it was magical. Mr. Bennett, Frida and I want to know what Milo Kuzniak did to kill Augustus Crane. Was it something in the land? Some spell or artifact? Crane might not have been Merlin, but he knew what he was doing, and still Kuzniak was able to not just defend himself, but kill Crane on top of it. No one's been able to figure it out."

Over a hundred years, and the incident was still a mystery—what made them think he could track it down? Ah—because he had a hundred-year-old magician along for the ride. Maybe he was better equipped than most. Call it magical archaeology.

He asked, "What happened to Kuzniak? Did anyone go after him for killing Crane?"

Judi shrugged. "He left town and disappeared. No one could prove that he'd done anything to kill Crane, but Crane's friends in town knew he must have done something and weren't at all happy. Lynch mobs still happened in those days, and ultimately his mining claim wasn't worth sticking around for. He died of a heart attack in Glenwood Springs about ten years later. Unrelated, near as anyone can figure."

Frida scowled, as if she could dismiss the whole thing, but she remained tense and stayed close to Judi. She said, "This area's full of ghost stories and tall tales. Some of Crane's friends were more than a little crazy—table-rapping Spiritualists. Crane may have just dropped dead of a heart attack, and they came up with this wacky story to make his death seem strange and mysterious. Do wizard duels like that even happen outside of books?"

"They do, once in a while." He'd been in a couple himself. He'd almost rather face off with six-shooters at high noon.

Judi said, "This would all just be a historical curiosity, but we're pretty sure someone's been poking around Kuzniak's old claim site. I leave the story off the tour for a reason—I don't want someone thinking they can learn what happened to Crane and maybe use that power themselves. You say you want what's in Amy's book to keep anyone else from getting hurt, and I believe you, Mr. Bennett."

"Call me Cormac," he said, because it seemed like the right thing to say. He didn't feel much like "Mr." anything.

"All right, Cormac. We'd like to learn what Kuzniak did in that duel, and what killed Crane, before someone else does. To keep anyone else from getting hurt, like you said. As someone who believes in fate, I can't help but think you came along for a reason."

"Yeah," he said, quirking a wry smile. "To ask about Amy Scanlon."

"You see? We can help each other."

He felt like he'd been tricked by a couple of grandmas, but couldn't figure out where the gotcha was. And really, he could just turn around and walk out.

They are setting us to investigating a murder that's over a hundred years old. Can we even do this?

We can try, he answered. What's one more mystery to take on, on top of all the others?

I'm not sure I trust them.

Then that puts us all on even ground.

Judi and Frida waited for his answer.

"I'd like to think it over. See if there's even enough to go on to track this down," he said, turning to leave. "I'll get out of your hair until then—"

"Wait—you never said how Amy passed away. Is there anything else you can tell me about what happened to her?" Judi leaned in, on the verge of reaching out to him.

He said, "No. I'm sorry. I wasn't there, it was my friend who was with her. I'm mostly doing all this for my friend."

The aunt said, "Is it possible—could I talk to this friend? I'd just like to know as much as I can. It's been over a year since I heard from Amy, and I just . . . I'd like to know."

He understood the request. What he didn't want was to drag Kitty back through that trauma—there was a reason he'd insisted he could do this on his own. He knew if he asked her to talk to Judi, Kitty would say yes. Best to let her make that decision, he supposed.

You could counter-bargain. Tell her Kitty will talk to her if she'll decode the book for us.

Cormac mentally shook his head. That wouldn't be right, when the woman was just looking for some closure.

"I'll see if she wants to talk," he said. "She may not want to."

"All right. Thank you."

He nodded at them and left the shop.

Chapter 5

AMELIA WAS familiar with the Spiritualist movement, which rose to prominence in the second half of the nineteenth century. More than familiar with it, she'd dabbled in it herself in her quest to learn everything she could about the occult, its practitioners, and the methods they used. The core idea of Spiritualism: through the guidance of a medium performing certain rituals, one might be able to communicate with spirits who have passed on. Primarily, people hoped to speak to loved ones and be assured of their comfort on "the other side." But others hoped to learn arcane secrets, to speak with great magicians and sages of the past, to gain power. Mostly, the only power these mediums displayed was the ability to dupe their clients and acquire their money.

Even when she was alive, she'd begun to hate the Spiritualists because, in general, they made her job harder. She couldn't simply follow stories of magic and ghosts and otherworldly monsters. No, she had to make judgments, don an air of skepticism, and investigate before she truly began investigating. Was this person making claims really a psychic communicating with dead spirits, or a charlatan cracking her toes under the table? It was all a supreme waste of time.

In her current experience, as a spirit who actually *had* passed on and returned, most people were less inclined to willingly speak with the dead than such beliefs would suggest. She'd tried for a century before finding someone able to listen to her—Cormac. Speaking with the dead in reality was not a safe parlor-bound activity, as the old Spiritualists insisted. No, in all the stories that had a seed of truth to them speaking with the dead required hardship and sacrifice, journeys to the underworld and copious amounts of blood.

Since meeting Cormac and coming back to life, she learned that the movement still existed in one form or another. She learned about the Cottingley Fairies and the great rivalry between Harry Houdini and Sir Arthur Conan Doyle over the photographs. The skeptical Mr. Houdini, Amelia decided, was a man she'd have very much liked to speak to, another reason to curse her early death that prevented such a meeting. But Sir Arthur believed utterly. Amelia thought the creator of the great Sherlock Holmes really should have known better. However, the First

World War and accompanying horrific loss of life had inspired a renewal of interest in Spiritualism. Sir Arthur had lost a son in the war. Amelia supposed she could forgive him for succumbing to an emotional response.

Amelia had started on her path because she desperately wanted to see fairies, exactly the kind of fairies that those little girls made cutout pictures of and posed in their garden. That alone should have raised doubts—the pictures were just what a late Edwardian little girl would imagine a fairy should look like, based on all the storybooks, paintings, and drawings surrounding her. Reality never matched expectations so precisely, in Amelia's experience. A hundred years ago, photography was still new enough that no one could believe that two young girls could falsify pictures. Photographs were the great truth-tellers, the artificial eye; they could not lie as paintings could. Except they could, and they had been made to lie from the very beginning. What would Sir Arthur make of the current era of computerized photo manipulation? How could one ever find the truth?

One simply had to keep looking, keep asking questions, and take nothing for granted.

THE DRIVE back to Denver seemed to take forever.

Do you know, Frida and Judi—I think they're together. As in a couple.

That had occurred to Cormac. He figured it was none of his business.

I had a spinster aunt, one of my mother's sisters, who lived with another spinster friend of hers. The family always spoke of how lovely it was that they got along so well and could live together with such economy without troubling their respective families. But there was much the family didn't say about them as well, and I wondered.

He got a hint of the memory as she rambled, an image of two dowdy middle-aged women standing arm in arm as if holding each other up, dressed all in black like they were shadows. They'd babysit sometimes, and Amelia remembered them teaching her croquet, when Amelia was young enough to wear her hair in pigtails tied up with big satin bows.

It seemed an alien world to Cormac, and he had nothing to say. But he suspected that, yes, there had been more to the women's relationship. The thought amused him, the two hiding behind propriety so stiff and formal that no one even questioned.

You know, he thought to Amelia, nobody says spinster anymore.

Well, yes, certainly. Etymologically, the word was doomed, considering so few of the women called spinsters actually spun wool anymore. So what do people call unmarried adult women now?

Um. Women, he said.

Ah.

He turned over the story Judi and Frida had told him. The old mystery intrigued him in spite of himself, but the magic was less interesting than the personalities involved. The egos. That's all it was in the end, clashing egos, and he was having trouble putting himself in that situation. There was a point where the only thing you were defending was your pride. He saw this kind of fight in prison all the time. Guys might call it fighting for dominance, to be top of the pecking order or to show some other asshole his place. But really, it was pride and not wanting to feel like anybody got the better of you.

Cormac figured out that he could walk away from those fights and his pride would survive just fine. He took care of his own pride, that wasn't anybody else's call. The petty fights and gang affiliations went on around him, and he didn't give a fuck. Everybody knew it, too. He bashed just enough heads to convince everyone to leave him alone. And they did.

But Kuzniak and Crane—two monumental egos, and what exactly had happened there at the end?

As of now, Cormac officially had too many mysteries to deal with. Too many questions needing answers. Hard to know where to start.

One book at a time. One call, one journey, one piece of the puzzle.

She was right. He started with the answer he could get right now, tucking his hands-free over his ear and making a call.

Kitty answered. "Hi. How'd it go?"

"How'd what go?"

"You said you were going to Manitou; I assume you're calling to tell me how it went. You find anything out?"

It hadn't occurred to him to call out of the blue to tell her how the meeting went. Mostly because he still didn't know how it was going to turn out. "No, not exactly. But I have a favor to ask." One in what was turning into a long chain of favors.

"Oh yeah?" What did it mean, that she actually sounded pleased at the prospect?

"Amy Scanlon's aunt wants to meet you. She wants to talk to the last person to see Amy alive."

A hesitation. "That's rough. I'm not sure I can tell her anything useful."

"I think she's just looking for a connection. The news about Amy seemed to hit pretty hard."

Kitty had a good heart. A big heart. If she thought she could help, she couldn't *not* help. That instinct had kept her as the alpha of the Denver werewolf pack the last several years. He felt like he was taking advantage.

"I'll talk to her," she said. "I'm happy talking to

her. And can I just say I told you, you should have let me come along from the start." She was smiling. Poking at him. He ignored her.

"We also need to talk about the book of shadows. Amy's aunt says she can interpret the code, and I think I believe her." *I believe her,* Amelia added. "We're pretty sure she's telling the truth. But she wants something in return."

"That's kind of fairy tale. What is it, you have to guess her real name or you have to give her your first-born?"

That . . . he never knew how to respond to her jokes.

"She wants me to solve a hundred-year-old murder."

"That sounds like . . . fun? Do you have a chance of actually solving it?"

"I'm mostly trying to decide if it'll be worth it. You think we can figure out the book of shadows without her help?"

"Her help would make it a lot easier. *If* she can help. Might not hurt to dig a little, just to see. I'm kind of curious."

"Then I'll start digging. See where it goes."

"Call me if there's anything else I can do."

"Yeah, will do." He clicked off, and boggled yet again at the reality of his current situation: he had backup. He was calling people to ask for help. And they were willing to give it, gratis. He'd opened himself up to Amelia, and he'd had to open himself to the rest of the world. His instinct was to shut it all back down. Flee to the hills, go back to what he knew.

Too late for that, I think.

That wasn't what bothered Cormac. Getting comfortable with it all—that was the weird part.

Chapter 6

KITTY FREED up her schedule the very next day and rode with Cormac down to Manitou Springs. She was uncharacteristically quiet during the trip, spending most of the time fidgeting, picking at her fingernails. Remembering, he expected. The disaster that had killed Amy Scanlon hadn't been all that long ago. Kitty's gaze had turned inward.

He found parking a block away and led her to the souvenir shop's front.

"This is it, huh?" she said, looking up at the MANITOU WISHING WELL sign overhead, arms crossed. Her hair was up in a sloppy ponytail, fringes of it hanging down around her ears and tanned cheeks. "Seems so ordinary. You say it's a couple of witchy types?"

"Something like that. Ready for this?"

She sighed. "Yeah."

A bell on the door rattled as they went inside. He watched her reaction—her nose flared, taking in scents, and she tilted her head and examined the space. Lupine movements, slightly odd if he hadn't been used to them by now.

"I suddenly want to buy everyone I know a T-shirt," she murmured, looking around at the collection, Colorado flags on pastels, lots of pictures of deer and columbine blooms. She gave a wry smile to one that showed a romanticized picture of a howling wolf, along with the words COLORFUL COLORADO. Wild wolves hadn't lived in the state for decades.

"I think they've got a spell on the place for that," he said.

Her brow furrowed. "Really? Nice."

The cat, Esther, was sitting on the glass counter again. When it saw Kitty, it arched its back, hissed loud enough to echo, then spun and dashed away. Kitty stared after it, blinking.

"Was that a cat? A hairless cat?" she said. "A hairless cat that evidently hates me?"

"She's a good judge of character," Frida said, emerging from the back room. She leaned both hands on the glass and nodded at him confrontationally. "You're a man with two auras and now you bring me a werewolf?"

Cormac hadn't remembered mentioning that about Kitty; of course, Frida could just see it.

"Hi," Kitty said, waving a hand. "Nice to meet you, too."

"Judi wanted to talk to her," Cormac said, then stepped out of the way.

"Who is it?" Judi asked, coming from the back of the store, feather duster in hand. "Wait a minute, I recognize you—aren't you the werewolf who shape-shifted on TV?"

Kitty turned to him. "See? We already know what the first line of my obituary is going to say."

He wished she wouldn't joke about obituaries.

When she looked back at the women, her smile was bright and amiable. The radio personality coming to the fore, a useful mask for situations like this. "I'm Kitty Norville. Cormac said you wanted to talk to me about Amy."

Both women seemed to deflate. Like they hadn't believed he would really bring Kitty to talk to them. She was the eyewitness, tangible proof that Judi's niece was well and truly gone.

"I'll go make some tea," Frida said softly. She glanced at Kitty, and her gaze fell. Frida squeezed Judi's hand as she passed by.

"We have some chairs, if you'd like to sit down." Judi led them toward the back of the shop, near the crystals and bookshelves, where she arranged a couple of folding chairs that had been tucked to the side. Kitty took the offered seat, and Judi sat across from her, but not too close—enough to read her face, not close enough to touch.

Cormac shook his head at a third chair and remained standing nearby, listening in but looking elsewhere. Wasn't his conversation, but he felt like he was standing guard.

Judi started: "He says you were with Amy when she died." Not a question, almost an accusation.

Kitty's smile was comforting, sad. "Not exactly. She was still alive when I left her. But we were in a cave, part of an old defunct mine up near Leadville. It collapsed while she was still inside. She . . . she knew she wasn't going to make it."

Kitty was very calm during this explanation. Cormac and Ben had arrived on the scene shortly after the cave-in—the noise of it, the rumble of a minor earthquake shuddering along the hillside, had drawn them to the location. She'd texted Ben, left a message with a GPS tag he'd been able to track, but the mine collapse had guided them the last hundred yards. Kitty had been missing for a week, and she'd looked like the survivor of some horror movie, coated with grime, torn clothes hanging off her, a wild look in her eyes. A starved wolf breaking out of a trap.

Hard to believe this was the same person. He'd been holding a rifle at the time, and a small corner of his mind had wondered if he'd have to shoot at her. When Ben arrived, she'd fallen into his arms, one of those beautiful scenes of reunion and love. He'd stepped aside, like usual.

Frida arrived with mugs of tea, gave one to Judi first, and Kitty accepted the next. She didn't offer one to Cormac, and that was fine.

"She caused the cave-in. I don't know exactly everything that happened, but there was a lot of magic involved. She and the people she was with were working a very powerful ritual. I was there because they kidnapped me, they needed a werewolf queen in order to work the spell—" She shook her head, as if she still hadn't made sense of it. "They opened a door, and a demon stepped through. Amy tried to banish it, but couldn't, so she brought down the cave to close the doorway on the thing. She didn't make it out, but two of us did. She saved our lives."

Judi gripped her mug and appeared dazed, as if she had just been informed about the death. "When I taught her, it was all charms, simple spells, nature magic. Nothing that would collapse a cave. What happened to her? These people she was with, this ritual—she knew better than to bother with anything that might summon a demon. What was she trying to do?"

"She was trying to save the world," Kitty said, straightforward, without irony. "She was kind of nuts. But she was brave." She took a sip of her tea, hiding her expression.

Cormac had a feeling Kitty was being kind, painting the girl in a better light than Cormac—or anyone else—would have. Probably for the best. Maybe her family would feel better remembering her as a hero. Didn't hurt anything.

Even Amelia was getting emotional. *I see so much of myself in Amy Scanlon, which makes no sense. It shouldn't be possible in a woman born in this era instead of mine. She had so many freedoms, so many opportunities . . . to have what she did and still yearn for more . . .*

You should talk to Kitty, he told her. Get a crash course in feminism. She'd tell you there's still plenty to yearn for.

I'm trying to decide . . . can I reasonably speculate about what Amy might have been thinking, simply based on my perception of our similarities? Or am I deluding myself that we had anything in common at all?

They'd just add it to the list of *maybes*.

"We think a lot of what she did was coded in her book of shadows," Kitty said, kindly but still leading in a subtle way Cormac never would have been able to manage. "I would love to know what she was thinking, before she got to where she ended up."

Judi shook a thought away and said, "So would I. She went to places I never thought of going. Never wanted to go. I'm not even sure what she was looking for."

Kitty wasn't a trained counselor, but she'd had plenty of practice playing amateur therapist on her radio show, and she obviously pulled those skills out now. "I've got her journal, her book of shadows. She told me to keep it, to use it. But we need the code to be able to do that. If you can help us with that, we'll give you the book, you can find out for yourself what she—"

"Oh, but I don't want that kind of magic," Judi said, smiling sadly. "And I must say I'm suspicious of you, that you do want it."

Kitty ducked her gaze, hiding amusement. "So you give Cormac a test, hand him this mystery and tell him to solve it, to see if he's worthy?"

"Is he?" Frida said bluntly, tipping her head at Cormac.

Cormac himself kind of wondered what Kitty was going to say to that.

She looked up at him, lips curled. "He does all right."

Then it was Kitty and Cormac looking back at the two of them. Kitty's brown-eyed gaze was so sympathetic, how could anyone tell her no?

The bell on the door rang, a customer entering, and Frida went to the cash register to help. The hairless cat reappeared, jumping on the counter to rub against the woman.

"You handed me a mystery," Cormac said. "I'm curious enough I'll take a look at it and let you know what I come up with, whether or not you want to help us with Amy's book. You can decide that later. How does that sound?"

Judi eased herself off the chair, collected Kitty's empty mug. "How can I argue with that?"

Kitty pulled a business card from her pocket. "Here's my number. If you want to talk any more about Amy, just call, any time."

Nodding, Judi accepted the card.

Then the meeting was over, and he and Kitty were back outside, walking on the sidewalk in the sunlight.

"Well," Kitty said. "Goodwill won, I think."

"So. You think she can help? Or is she stringing me along?"

Mouth pursed, she thought a moment. "They just . . . Judi at least has a memory of Amy that doesn't match up with the Amy I knew. That has to be hard. They want to be careful, I think. Neither one of them made my hackles twitch, if that helps. Well, that cat did. Yeesh. Don't trust that cat, okay?"

It was as good a vote of confidence as he was likely to get.

Chapter 7

FROM WHAT little the two women had given him, Cormac had a surprising amount of information to go on: the names of the people involved, newspaper articles about the event, the location where the so-called wizards' duel had taken place. And Amelia's memories.

I never met Augustus Crane, but I heard about him. She's right, Manitou Springs was filled with ghost hunters and Spiritualists back then. Hobbyists, mostly. Well-to-do folk looking for a thrill, trying to be daring. Crane was a bit more serious—he was a mentor to many who still mourned his loss when I arrived in the area. Some claimed his ghost haunted the bit of land where he'd died. People would speak of Crane's rival without ever mentioning his name. This must be Milo Kuzniak. For my part, the brand of magic practiced by him and his followers was too public and full of artifice for me to pay much mind.

Too many frauds manipulating the gullible. I had other interests.

Amelia had never been interested in showing off; she was interested in power. She didn't care what others thought of her. She wanted to know how magic worked. All of it.

One of the old newspaper archives included a photo of Crane; he looked exactly the way Cormac imagined a late nineteenth-century upper-class gentleman and dabbler in magic would look like, standing tall in front of a gazebo, dressed in a crisp pale suit and striped tie, clean shaven, hat on his head, pocket watch visible. He had a smug assurance about him, and didn't smile. The caption in the newspaper clipping said this had been taken at a garden party held by one of the local families.

There were no pictures of Milo Kuzniak. He seemed to have been most interested in getting rich. Made him an easy guy to figure out.

Cormac decided to start the hunt where Milo Kuzniak made his old mining claim, the same place he'd faced off with and killed Augustus Crane.

A day of digging in records and checking topographic maps confirmed the location.

Map and GPS reader in hand, he parked his Jeep in a turnoff on one of the dirt roads leading into the hills from Highway 24. The vehicle looked way more at home here than it did in any parking lot. It had ten years of mud caking the wheel wells; sun had faded the brown to tan. The windshield had a dozen star-shaped dings in it, the sides had a couple of noticeable dents and a few angry scratches in the paint. One set of scratches, three horizontal lines running across the hard top then down the side, came from a werewolf that had jumped on and slid off. Battle scars. The Jeep suited him.

He started walking. Winter was winding down; it had been a couple of weeks since the last snow, which had mostly melted away. A few drifts and pockets of packed snow remained in the shadows of rocks, in dirt-rimmed depressions. A cold breeze blew, and he was happy to wear his jacket.

East of here, red sandstone slabs tipped vertical, creating windblown formations like the ones found in Garden of the Gods. The further west you got, the further into the mountains, granite replaced sandstone. Scrub oak and pine forests grew scattered over a dry landscape, cut through with gullies and rock outcroppings. Early prospectors found flakes and nuggets of gold and silver just washing out of these hills. Now, the remaining gold ore lay in veins thousands of feet underground and mining was an industrial operation. Out by Cripple Creek, mining companies were taking off entire mountaintops to get to the gold.

There were easier ways to make a living.

Amazingly, this particular area was still wild. A

dozen miles or so northwest of the town, it had been incorporated into the Pike National Forest and left alone, too rocky and inaccessible to easily develop. Cormac suspected this was part of what had drawn Milo here. There hadn't been any roads up here a hundred years ago, and there weren't any now. Someone would have needed a burro and a lot of patience to get anything more than themselves to the sloping, precarious claim.

The hillside was steep; Cormac braced on trees and boulders as he made his way up, and each step sent a rain of loose dirt and pebbles sliding down. A path did wind its way through here, a paler strip along in the ground. Hikers and hunters might have frequented the spot. Kids looking for a place to get drunk and make out. This might have been the same burro trail Milo had followed on his way to his claim, worn into the rock.

The trail leveled off to a small plateau, maybe fifty yards across, bound by a narrow ridge on one side, sloping down into the next valley on the other. He checked the GPS and confirmed, this was it. The pines here were small, gnarled by the wind, which must have blown pretty much constantly. A handful of birds, chickadees it sounded like, flitted in a stand of scrub oak. Blowing grit rattled against his sunglasses.

Surely anything he might have left here will be long gone, Amelia observed.

Cormac took a slow walk around the site anyway, tipping up rocks with his boots, checking under trees for anything out of place. Didn't even find a broken beer bottle or weather-faded can, which meant nobody came up here much. At least, nobody stopped for long if they did. He wondered if bringing a metal detector up here would uncover anything.

He took a moment to stand still, listening. Waiting for that prickling on the back of his neck that told him something strange was close by, a feeling of warning that had as much to do with instinct as anything supernatural.

Let's scry a bit, see if anything turns up.

Since meeting Amelia and leaving prison, he'd taken to carrying a collection of items in his pockets. String, a candle stub, a packet of salt, a few herbs like sage and rowan. A piece of chalk, a bit of iron, a quartz crystal. The most basic tools of spell casting. He could work just about any kind of basic magic with these items. Rather, Amelia could work magic, using his body to manipulate the items, to power the spells. She'd been able to use her magic to preserve her soul, but without a body, she couldn't use what she'd learned.

Over time, Cormac had come to see the usefulness of Amelia's brand of magic. Made up a little for losing his guns—though as he sometimes joked at Ben, it wasn't having guns that was strictly illegal for a convicted felon like him; it was getting caught with them. Ben didn't think that was funny.

This is quite simple, really. It won't tell us details, but it will tell us if this location has a strong magical presence or not. This might indicate if Kuzniak used magic to kill Crane.

"Let's get to it then."

First, face east. Then we'll need a small hole in the ground—

He found east by the sun, which was edging past noon to the western hills, then found a sheltered space where he dug a divot in the ground using his boot heel.

We need kindling for a fire, and a match—

Using his pocket knife, he cut a twig and its lingering dried-up leaves from a scrub oak and crumbled the vegetation into the hole. Early discussions between them established that a disposable lighter worked just as well as a match. Better, even, though it might not have been as elegant and mysterious. Amelia was still getting used to the wondrous modern technology.

In the end, he could only do so much, following the easy directions she gave him. He could do the prep work, the hard labor. But just about every spell had a moment where timing and precision came into the mix. A deeper knowledge, the kind of thing Amelia had spent her life studying, and Cormac hadn't. So he gave himself over to Amelia.

In that moment, he didn't have control of his body.

He was there looking through his eyes, he could feel his thumb resting on the lighter, felt the sun's heat on the back of his neck, but Amelia was doing the moving. Wasn't quite an out-of-body experience. More like sitting in the passenger seat when you didn't know if the person next to you could really drive. He'd learned to sit back calmly, resting in the back of his own mind so he didn't panic and freeze up.

Kitty told him once that he'd fallen asleep, but Amelia hadn't, and talked in a dreamlike state. He didn't remember that. He wouldn't say that he was afraid she'd up and take him over entirely one of these days, waiting until he fell asleep and then going for some walk he wouldn't appreciate. But nervous wasn't quite afraid, was it?

I wouldn't do that, she commented. *When you sleep, I sleep.* I *was talking in* your *sleep, that time.*

That didn't even make sense.

She held up the lighter and a length of red string, then whispered an incantation with his voice, something in a language he didn't know, probably Latin but knowing Amelia it could have been anything. She repeated the incantation twice more, set the string on fire, and dropped it in the makeshift cauldron filled with leaves.

The vegetation instantly caught and flared in a foot-high burst of flame that made Cormac sit back. In a moment, the leaves were nothing but ashes, and the edges of the shallow dish in the soil were scorched.

Amelia gave a mental shiver that might have been a deep sigh. "That's good enough, I think."

It felt like an extra long blink, a brief moment of vertigo, and she fell into the back of his mind. He was at the fore, right where he belonged, without even thinking of it, like nothing had happened. Back in control of his body, Cormac brushed himself off and looked around to make sure they hadn't set anything on fire.

"I take it that's a positive," he murmured.

Oh, I would very much say so.

A noise—footsteps—caught Cormac's ear, and a male voice shouted at them from the head of the trail. "Hey, you! You there! Stand up! Keep your hands up!"

He looked over his shoulder to see a man standing some thirty yards away, holding a rifle pointed at him.

Chapter 8

CORMAC STILL held the lighter. He kept it in sight, putting both his hands up while he slowly got to his feet, stamping out the last of the smoldering ashes. So, this must have been the guy poking around Judi and Frida had mentioned.

There were actually four guys, three with guns, but only the guy in the middle had drawn on him. The other two who were carrying waited to see what their alpha male buddy would do, and if Cormac was going to give them any trouble. The fourth guy stood behind the others, hunched in a long overcoat and looking miserable. Cormac kept his eyes on the armed trio while mentally reviewing the area and his escape routes. He couldn't win in a fight with all three of them, but there was enough cover here he could avoid getting shot. If he had to, he could go over the edge of the plateau and slide to safety on his ass without getting himself too badly hurt. Though his recently broken and healed arm throbbed at the memory of how well that sort of thing usually went.

He nudged Amelia. You got anything that can spook these guys?

Nothing that's faster than they can fire on us.

"Cormac Bennett?"

When the man lowered the rifle from his shoulder, Cormac recognized him. "Anderson Layne," he answered, without enthusiasm.

He hadn't seen the man in more than a decade. Guy must have been in his forties now, his buzz cut more gray than brown, but he had the same glare and the same gnarled set to his limbs, big knuckles gripping the rifle, broad shoulders showing through his heavy tan hunting jacket. He was someone who worked out compulsively, a big guy who knew his strength, but was trying not to notice he was getting older.

Cormac cursed to himself. Out of all the places and times he could have run into Anderson Layne, it had to be here, and now. On the other hand, Layne seemed happy to see him. Maybe Cormac should have expected this. Knowing these guys was either going to make this easier or harder.

Laughing, Layne tucked the rifle under his arm, which was only mildly comforting.

"Jesus, how long's it been? How you doing?" He strode forward, hand outstretched to shake, and Cormac walked up to meet him. "You guys remember

Cormac? Douglas Bennett's kid? Who'd have figured it, running into you out here?"

Layne had been part of the bunch headed up by David O'Farrell, Ben's father. Militia and sovereignty activists playing at being freedom fighters, mostly using it as an excuse to collect automatic weapons and blow shit up. Cormac had been mixed up with them in his late teens—they had access to guns, and they had connections. Everybody seemed to know his father, and Cormac had gotten his first few jobs through those contacts. When Ben went away to college, then law school, Cormac drifted away from his increasingly unbalanced uncle. Ben had seen the writing on the wall and tried to get his father to give up the movement. David O'Farrell didn't take the warning, declaring instead that his son had been suckered by the government and was a fool for following the rules. On the other hand, Cormac did take the warning, because Ben wasn't stupid, and he turned out to be right. When his uncle had been arrested on a catalog of conspiracy charges, the group had scattered. Cormac hadn't seen them in over a decade, and he didn't miss them at all. He shook Layne's hand anyway.

The other two might have been part of that bunch, back in the day. Cormac hadn't known everyone, or hadn't bothered remembering everyone. They were closer to his age than Layne's. Layne's protégés, just as Layne had been David's. And the beat went on.

Cormac nodded at them and said, "Been awhile."

"So," Layne said, questioningly, studiously. "What are you doing out here?"

"Oh, taking a walk, checking things out. Heard some ghost stories about the spot, wanted to see for myself."

"You want to see ghosts, shouldn't you be out here at midnight?"

"Depends on the ghost. What about you? Coming up here to shoot cans or something?"

Layne's smile might have gotten stiffer at that. "Where are you these days, still up in Greeley? You have time to go get a drink? I think we might be able to help each other."

He very much didn't want to go drink with Anderson Layne. Just seeing the guy standing there felt like fishhooks from his old life biting into him, trying to drag him off. But Layne being here might mean he knew something. This was the next signpost on the trail. In the end, he was still standing between Cormac and the way out, holding a gun.

Cormac agreed to the drink.

THEY RECONVENED in a run-down biker bar off Highway 24 just outside of Woodland Park. Cormac gathered that it was a regular haunt of Layne's and his bunch. The bartender, a tall, skinny white guy with a beard and tattoos peeking out from under his shirt collar, waved when they came in and greeted Layne by name. After coming in from the bright afternoon, Cormac paused a moment to take off his sunglasses and let his vision adjust to the darker interior, lit by a few overhead lights and sun coming in through a tinted front window. The place was cheap, cheap-looking, fully by intention, with a concrete floor and stale, beer-tinged air. Wood paneling on the walls was decorated with lots of neon beer ads and posters for old promotions, like last season's Broncos football schedule. A Confederate flag hung on the back wall as some sort of test—if it offended you, you probably shouldn't be here. He ducked his head to hide a smile at the predictability of it all.

Layne brazened in like he owned the place and couldn't be at all subtle. He hauled himself onto a barstool and announced, "Hey, Dan! Guess who I found? It's Cormac Bennett—you know, Douglas Bennett's kid. The vampire hunter! You're still into that weird shit, aren't you?"

About as subtle as dynamite. Bartender Dan stretched out his hand for Cormac to shake, which he did as he joined Layne at the bar.

"It's not as exciting as it sounds," Cormac said. "Not like in the movies."

"And I'm sure you're just being modest," Layne insisted. "You know, you might not believe this, but I was just thinking of calling you. I might have a job for you."

Dan put bottles in front of them, and Cormac sipped. People kept offering him jobs—why didn't he feel lucky? "Yeah?" Curt, noncommittal.

"How much have you heard about that spot on the plateau?"

Cormac decided to hold out some bait, do some fishing. "Back a hundred or so years ago, a prospector staked a claim up there and ran into trouble. Stories say he killed someone. Stories don't say whether he ever found any gold."

"Yeah, I know those stories. Kind of like the ones about your dad. I mean, we all heard about him going after weird shit—werewolves, vampires, you know?—but this was years ago and we all thought that was bullshit, just crazy stories to make him come off even scarier than he was. But then—well, it was all true, wasn't it? And we heard all the stories about how you picked up where he left off, hunting monsters." He had a disturbing gleam in his eyes.

Cormac didn't have a clue what those stories looked like from the outside, or what someone like Layne saw in them. "That was a long time ago. I haven't been hunting in years."

Layne clearly didn't believe him. That grin suggested they were both in on a secret. "Can I ask you something? What if I wanted to get in on that? I figure there are a lot more of them than we ever thought. If you're not hunting them anymore—teach me to do it. I'll get in on the action."

The thought of someone like Layne going after Kitty and Ben made Cormac want to shoot the bastard. And this was why it was probably just as well he didn't carry a gun anymore.

"Why?" Cormac said flatly, first thing to come into his head. Might even have been Amelia who said it.

Layne shrugged like it was obvious. "Someone's got to. The more the better, right? It's them or us."

In the space of about a second Cormac thought up, mulled over, worked out, and then rejected a plan to agree to teach Layne how to hunt the supernatural—and then teach him flat-out wrong, so that the first time the guy went up against a vampire or lycanthrope it would be sure to end very badly for him.

"You know," he said, "Some of my best friends are werewolves." Layne chuckled, clearly not sure whether or not he had just made a joke, so Cormac moved on. "Tell me about what's up on that plateau. You hunting vampires up there?"

Layne's grin went feral. "Let me introduce you to the man who's going to make things happen." He pointed to the sullen man of the group, still hunched up in his coat like he was out in the cold. He glared back at Cormac. "Cormac, this is Milo Kuzniak."

Cormac's first thought: the guy was a vampire. Milo Kuzniak had been in his thirties over a century ago, he couldn't still be alive—unless he was a vampire. But the broad daylight outside said no, he wasn't, unless he'd come up with a way to make himself immune to daylight. Now there was an unhappy thought.

Or maybe Cormac had been spending too much time with monsters.

It's a coincidence. Has to be, Amelia thought.

He hadn't found any pictures of the old prospector Kuzniak and couldn't guess if this guy, who appeared to be in his late twenties, had any physical resemblance to him. He had dark hair cut short and a round face, crooked teeth, and a hungry look in his eyes. Even hungrier than Layne.

"I knew another guy named Kuzniak once. You from around here?" Cormac said, offhand, because he had to say something.

The guy licked his lips as if thinking, maybe wondering if he was giving anything away. "Yes. My great-grandfather homesteaded out here. I'm named after him."

A perfectly reasonable, normal explanation. "You inherit anything else from him?"

He gave a lopsided shrug. "This and that. You really hunt vampires?"

"Once or twice."

Kuzniak donned a contemptuous grin. "There's no vampires around here."

"Then I'll leave the garlic and holy water at home," he said. Given the kind of company Kitty and Ben kept, he always had a stake at hand, tucked into a pocket inside the sleeve of his jacket. If he really wanted to be a jackass he could slip it out, twirl it around his fingers a couple of times, make some kind of threat. But this was all just posturing. Instead he said, "You're going after the gold, aren't you?"

Kuzniak's expression shut down, and he looked to Layne, who just smiled. "See? I told you, the guy's smart. Worth having on our side. I'm telling you, Douglas Bennett's kid—he'll know things. He can help."

"I know everything we need," Kuzniak argued.

"If that was true, we'd be done with it all already, wouldn't we?"

This pit was getting deeper and deeper. Cormac had the thought that maybe he should just walk away. It wasn't too late.

If he knows what the first Milo Kuzniak knew, then he might know what killed Crane. We stay. Cormac guessed that Amelia wasn't even thinking about passing the information along to Judi and Frida—she wanted to know, all for herself.

"What about it, Bennett? You in?"

"For a cut, I assume," he answered.

"Sure. Even cut like the rest of us. Assuming you can do the job I've got in mind for you."

That meant all the rest of the gang's cuts just shrank, and none of them looked happy about it. Likely, Layne was pitting them against each other. A little friendly competition among subordinates looking for promotion. This was exactly why Cormac preferred working alone.

This ought to be fun. "I'll see what I can do."

Layne's two heavies went to play pool at a crappy, beat up pool table. The younger Kuzniak moved down the bar, glaring at Cormac like he was planning what curse to cast on him, and Cormac was thinking it was about time he got out of here. But Layne kept staring at him. Hero worship, just about.

"What?" he finally said to Layne.

"It's fate, you know. Fate that I'd run into Douglas Bennett's kid, right here and now."

Second time in as many days someone evoked fate at him. He didn't think much of fate's judgment.

"I've heard my dad's name more in the last hour than I have in the last ten years."

"He's a legend, you know that."

Yes, he did. But only in circles like this. The man had died more than half Cormac's lifetime ago. There'd been a time all he wanted in life was to make the man proud. He'd been desperate to make his dead father proud, and horrified to think Douglas Bennett would be disappointed instead. Every time Cormac missed a shot, he imagined his father was looking down on him, shaking his head.

At some point—maybe in prison—Cormac was able to look back and think maybe his father didn't matter so much. He'd been a man, he'd made mistakes. He'd been single minded, obsessive. He'd died young, violently, like Cormac assumed would happen to him. Until he decided that maybe it didn't have to go that way, and that maybe Douglas Bennett had been wrong about the monsters.

"That was a long time ago," he said. He'd only gotten halfway through the beer and didn't plan on finishing. The stuff tasted warm and musty. He pushed the bottle away.

Layne said, "We're all getting together in a couple of days—I could really use your help. You want to know more, come out to my place. Give me your number, I'll call you."

It was ominous, but it was a lead. Cormac gave his number, and Layne entered it into his phone.

He didn't feel the need to keep being chummy with the group, so he pushed off from the table. "I'd better get going. Leave you boys to it. Interesting running into you."

"I'll be in touch."

Cormac gave a sloppy wave in reply. He needed to keep track of Layne. Just to keep an eye on these guys.

He threw open the bar's front door and marched into the parking lot, more distracted than he should have been because he almost ran into a woman who was coming the other way. They stopped, stared at each other for a moment, blinking. She was in her thirties, brown hair in a short ponytail, dressed in practical jeans and blue winter coat. Tired around the eyes, minimal makeup.

He didn't even have to think about it to remember her name, it just popped out. "Mollie. Mollie Layne."

She smiled and might even have looked pleased. "Cormac Bennett! Oh my God, it's been a long time, hasn't it? And it's Mollie Cramer now. And for the last fifteen years." She shrugged as if apologizing.

It had been close to twenty years since he'd seen her. Had it been that long? He didn't have a clue she'd gotten married—why should he? "Sure. Well, a late congratulations, I guess."

"Yeah—and divorced now. Two kids, single mom, the works. Who'd have thunk?"

Christ, he was eighteen and awkward all over again. Fifteen years—more than enough time for a marriage, divorce, and two kids. She might have been about twenty pounds heavier, but he recognized the teenage girl he'd known in the woman she'd turned into.

The big smile, the fall of brown hair. But he didn't know what to say to her.

"What've you been up to?" she asked.

He shoved his hands into his jacket pocket. "This and that, I guess. Just passing through. Funny, running into you."

"Yeah—but good, you know? I figured the way you were going back in the day you'd end up doing yourself in in a blaze of glory. I'm glad you didn't."

"Thanks."

"Is my brother in there?"

"Anderson? Yeah. I ran into him up on the mountain. It's a day for reunions, I guess."

She rolled her eyes. "The kids are with their dad this week; I'm supposed to head down to his house and help him clean but he hasn't given me a key. Now there's someone who has *not* gotten his shit together."

They spent another long moment studying each other. He sorted through a bunch of memories he hadn't thought about in a long time, and wasn't sure what to think about them now.

"Well, I'd better get going, I guess," she said, skirting around him to continue on to the door.

"Yeah, me too. Good running into you." He even meant it. She shoved Layne and his schemes and every other problem he had to solve straight out of his mind.

"Yeah. I like the mustache, Cormac. It's all Marlboro Man. Kinda cool."

"See you, Mollie." And that was that, she was inside, the door closing behind her.

He sat in his Jeep for a good minute, just taking it in, but then hurried to start the engine and peel back onto the highway before she came back out to the parking lot and he had to figure out what else to say.

And what was all that about? Amelia had been very quiet through the encounter.

"That was Mollie."

And who is Mollie?

Amelia caught a whole tumble of images and memories that Cormac couldn't lock up fast enough. *You had carnal relations with her!* She sounded scandalized.

Not just that, she'd been the first girl Cormac ever slept with. They'd been seventeen, both of them virgins fumbling in the loft of the O'Farrell's main barn when the adults were off at some event or other. But they'd managed and carried on for a few months after that. He couldn't remember anymore who'd broken up with whom. They'd graduated and gone their separate ways. He seemed to think that maybe he'd stopped calling her before she'd stopped calling him. But he couldn't think of why. He couldn't see inside that screwed-up kid's head anymore. Just as well.

It occurred to him, now that he was twenty miles down the highway, that he could have asked for her phone number. He was kind of glad he hadn't thought of it. He probably wouldn't see her again.

I will never understand you, Cormac Bennett.

Not like that was a surprise.

Chapter 9

ONE THING Amelia and Cormac had in common: nothing surprised her anymore. She'd started by looking for fairies, and she'd found so much more. She'd made it around the world before arriving in Manitou Springs and meeting her end. She'd learned so much, encountered so much. Never enough, of course. But at least she was rarely surprised anymore. Not by vampires or werewolves, not by magicians' duels, not by anything.

She remembered when she first learned that vampires and werewolves were real.

She had just left home for the last time a few months before, after burning all her bridges with her family, after she'd declined Arthur Pembroke's proposal and had that terrible row with her brother. If they were going to be disappointed and ashamed of her, she would earn their ill will.

Looking back on it, she'd been very young, very

naïve, and hadn't known quite where to start in her investigations of the veiled world. She had no other choice but to start where almost everyone started—with the stories. Which led her to Romania, because like so many others at that time, she'd read *Dracula* and wondered how much of it was real. It had just been published, and she carried a copy of it with her on the ferry out of Dover. In her second life, she could weep over how much that first edition would be worth if she still had it.

She had launched her own Grand Tour of Europe, visiting Templar castles and prehistoric dolmens, seeking out Romany fortune tellers and Theosophists who held court at salons in the various capitals. The hardest part was convincing them that she was serious, and that she would not be satisfied with parlor tricks. She revealed her own fairy charms and old Celtic protective magic. She feared that most thought her just another silly English girl taken in by fanciful tales. She encountered much chaff in her search for grains of power. But she did find them, and she went to find the seed of truth at the heart of Bram Stoker's novel.

A young woman could travel alone in the late Victorian world if she had a good story to explain herself, a ready line of credit, a dictatorial confidence in her dealings with others, and a sturdy umbrella or walking stick. She had all of these. She told people she was a scholar from a well-to-do family, which was entirely true, but she also told them she had her family's blessing, and by extension their protection. She had a line she used: that in a world where a queen ruled the most successful empire on Earth, couldn't a woman be expected to travel alone safely? This at least made people stop to consider her.

Usually, though, they were astonished enough at her demeanor and questions that they seemed to remove her from the category of "woman" entirely. The irony of surviving into a world where she could travel nearly anywhere without enduring endless questioning about "where is your husband/father/brother?" was that she was now housed within the body of a man and it all became moot.

Bucharest was splendid and modern, and she stayed for a month in a little pension operated by a German widow. She read books in the libraries, questioned professors about local history, and listened for stories of vampires. She learned about Vlad the Impaler of course, and also about Countess Báthory, who was said to have murdered over six hundred girls and bathed in their blood to retain her youth. This story itself planted the seed that led to developing the spell she eventually used to preserve her soul within the walls of the Colorado Territorial Correctional Facility. The spell had nothing to do with blood and youth, of course, but Amelia became intrigued by the idea of preservation, of using magic to ensure a person might live on. In the end, she had not used the spell in the manner she expected to at all, but she couldn't complain. She was still here, in a manner of speaking.

It was all very sensationalist. The stories focused on what one would expect the popular imagination to focus on: the dream of eternal youth, shocking violence, and vast quantities of spilled blood.

With a collection of tales and threads of inquiry in hand, she went into the rural areas, the forests and mountains and villages that hadn't changed in centuries. She could feel mysteries seeping up from the ground, charging the very air, beckoning her.

She procured a room at a village's lone pension and found herself in the tavern next door, very much like one Jonathan Harker might have patronized in the story. She ordered what passed for an ale in this locale, a hearty stew, and wrote in her journal of what she had found: the gods and spirits said to live in the hills, local charms, protective symbols carved into the lintels over doorways in barns—in the doorway at this very pub, the wheel-and-circle symbol called the *gromoviti znaci,* which protected against storms.

Night fell. A man just shy of middle age came into the tavern and sat at the table next to hers. She was aware of his presence, and aware of her umbrella propped at her chair. A glance told her that the proprietor had left for a moment, but there were two others in the room, a pair of travelers bent over their meal in the corner. She would not have paid any more attention to this newcomer, except that he was watching her. After what seemed a very long time of this, she turned to him with a raised eyebrow, questioning.

"You are very intent on your writing," he said. He spoke with the sort of precise accent typical of someone who'd been born in another country but educated in England. He'd erased evidence of his origins from that accent. "Might I inquire what it is you write?"

"I am a bit of a scholar," she said with a thin smile. "I've been investigating local folklore practices."

He had an olive complexion, but pale, as if he spent most of his time indoors. Clean shaven, he was well dressed in a tailored coat and silk cravat with a gold and diamond pin in it. He might have been a merchant or high-ranking official of some kind.

"Oh, please do not tell me you've been taken in by that Irish novelist. You do not seem the kind of young woman to read such drivel."

"I'll read anything," she said. "You've read *Dracula,* then?"

"You are not the first to come traveling here looking for the truth of Stoker's monster."

She had to hide some disappointment. She had thought people's annoyance with her had to do with her sex. Setting down her pen, she turned to him, shifting her disappointment to amusement, making a joke of it. "Do any of them find what they're looking for? Do you believe that vampires exist?"

"I don't have to believe it," he said. "I know they do. And they are very much as dangerous as Stoker writes of. You should be careful."

She had no reason to believe him. He was simply a fellow traveler making a joke. But something of his seriousness, his intensity—her impulse was to believe him, even if she could not catch his gaze to look him in the eyes to judge him. This should have made him seem evasive, untrustworthy. Instead, it made him seem sad.

"Are there very many of them about?" she said, with a newspaper journalist's detached curiosity. "Or are they rare—a single master with a handful of progeny, as in the novel?"

"Both, I would say. It depends greatly on where you are. Do keep in mind, such rural environs as this aren't well suited to vampires, who need a ready supply of living souls in order to survive. They are parasites, after all, with all that implies."

She hadn't thought of vampires in those terms, a parasite like a remora or mistletoe, but the description seemed apt. She became even more curious.

Her reticule was on the table beside her. She tugged open the drawstring and drew out the silver cross, as long as her fingers, that she kept there. Setting it on the table, she slid it toward the man, watching his reaction.

He stared at it, but did not flinch. She wasn't sure why she thought he might.

"I'm given to understand this serves as protection."

"It does. Sometimes."

This seemed ominous. "You seem knowledgeable on this topic—confident—which leads me to believe you can help me. I would like to meet a vampire. I have so many questions."

She kept trying to meet his gaze, to hold to it, to judge his character, to learn if he was lying or not. That he kept his eyes downcast suggested he was untrustworthy. A coward, even, with some ulterior motive to trick or rob her. But that lingering sadness about him threw her entirely into doubt.

"I would advise against it. I fear I must be going, but speaking with you has been a pleasant diversion. Have a good evening, miss. And do be careful." He stood, gave a short bow, and departed.

He had never ordered any food or drink.

That night was a full moon, and from her room she heard the howls of wolves in the distance. When she asked the innkeeper about them, he said they were pests and that hunters were slowly culling the region's wolf population. We would all be so much safer when they were gone, he said.

The setting she traveled through for the next month was sufficiently beautiful and intriguing to make her journey worthwhile, but she decided that one location was not any more likely to play host to vampires than any other, and so continued on to Istanbul. She thought about the mysterious man in the tavern often, but still was not sure she'd ever met a vampire. At least, not until she entered Cormac's world. From him, she learned that vampires had a power they exerted through their gaze, a subtle hypnotic mind control, and that it was best to never make eye contact with them. Cormac wore dark glasses when any of Kitty's vampire friends came around, to prevent them from catching his gaze.

The gentleman in the tavern had been protecting her. Her memory of his specific features had faded over time. She remembered the incident more than the man, and so could not show Cormac an image of him or describe him well enough to learn if Kitty recognized him. But she liked to think the man still existed somewhere, and that she might meet him again someday.

What she'd learned about vampires, lycanthropes, skinwalkers, wizards, people who simply dabbled in magic or those whose entire existence was submerged in the supernatural—they'd all started out as people, which meant they could be understood as people. Their motivations, fears, desires—comprehensible. They only seemed mysterious—and mysteries could be solved.

Chapter 10

CORMAC GOT back home past dark and collapsed into bed. Fell into a half sleep, and from there he dreamed of the meadow, and of the woman in a long skirt and high-collared shirt. It was like she'd been waiting for him.

They walked side by side along the creek, wading through knee-high grass. Her skirts made a shushing, brushing sound as she passed. Overhead, a hawk called as it soared from one end of the valley to the other. Cormac watched it, calmly astonished. Every time they came here, he found more details, from a bee buzzing at a wildflower to the gray-green lichens painting the rocks. It all seemed so real. And impossible.

"You don't trust them," Amelia started the conversation by stating the obvious. "You want to know what they're doing, but you don't trust them."

"What I really want to know—why's a guy like

Anderson Layne suddenly interested in hunting monsters? I know he knew my dad, but it's not like they were best friends. They moved in the same circles back in the day but it's not like they were drinking buddies. He hung out more with my uncle. He said it himself, he thought it was all bunk until the publicity started a few years ago."

"It's quite obvious, isn't it? He's interested in hunting monsters because he has a monster he needs to kill."

Layne had been jumpy, up on that hillside. If he'd found some random stranger poking around, he'd have had no problem threatening them, including firing off a round or two, to scare them off. He was guarding that patch from someone. Something more than a fellow lowlife thug, then? Vampire or lycanthrope? Well, that was just what Cormac needed in the mix, wasn't it?

He ran a hand over his hair, grimacing at the distant hills. "Yeah, figured."

"Whatever Anderson Layne's situation is—surely between the two of us we can manage it. Especially for the sake of learning what Kuzniak knows."

"What Kuzniak knows—about how his great-grandfather killed Crane, or about how to get gold out of those rocks?"

She offered a thin smile. "Yes?"

If you were going to spend your time thinking out

loud, this was the way to do it. Cormac knew how to track monsters. Working out more complicated problems like this—it helped to have an extra perspective. And it felt so *real*. He could see her chest, the fabric of her blouse moving in and out as she breathed. She was dead, she didn't need to breathe. . . .

They stopped, facing each other by the running water of the creek. She said, "If there was ever gold on that claim, it's still there because no one has any indication that Kuzniak ever got it out. Kuzniak must have passed on his knowledge to his descendants."

Cormac continued the thought. "He never even dug, there's no sign on that plateau of there ever being a mine—"

"Because he was a magician. He had some magical ability. Was he trying to find a way to bring the gold out of the ground magically?"

Her expression turned bemused, wondering—mirroring his own slack face, he was sure. "You'd think if that was possible someone would have done it by now. Lots of people would have done it by now, and gotten stupidly rich at it."

"There really aren't that many magicians in the world, and not that much magic, despite your proximity to so much of it," Amelia said. "Such a thing wouldn't go unnoticed, and most magicians I've known preferred anonymity over wealth."

"But a guy like Anderson Layne—"

"If there's a way to use magic to pull gold from the ground, he does seem like someone who would be interested, yes."

He wiped his hand over his chin, thinking. "So does he? Have a way to pull gold from the ground?"

"We'll have to keep playing along if we want to find out. Are you all right with that?" Her eyes were crinkled against the sun—another odd detail that set him off balance, like it was too much detail for him to just be thinking it up. It made him imagine she was more than a ghost, a spirit in his mind. They weren't here, this wasn't real. But it sure felt like it.

"Yeah, it's just the next step on the path."

"Ben won't be happy with you if he knows you're in contact with your old crowd."

"Then he won't have to know about it, will he?"

"That always goes so well," she murmured. "And now, I would like you to tell me about Mollie Layne." She didn't manage the innocent smile she seemed to be trying for.

"Mollie Cramer, she said."

"And?"

"And what?"

"There's history between you. I'm simply curious."

It was none of her business, he thought, staring into the woods on the other side of the creek, thinking he might see deer there. She might have been living inside his head, but he deserved some kind of privacy.

"What you deserve and what we have here are two different things," she said. Her voice had turned sad, her expression withdrawn. She looked away.

"It was a long time ago. Twenty years. We were just kids."

"But you still find her attractive? If you had an opportunity . . ."

"Better if I don't. Not while we're working with Layne." But he'd thought about it. What Amelia was politely not saying was how he hadn't slept with anyone since before prison. Not that he'd ever had anything resembling a relationship, not like Ben and Kitty had. But he'd had plenty of opportunities. And now . . . seeing Mollie reminded him that it had been a long time.

"You'll see her again, perhaps," Amelia said. She was trying to be comforting, Cormac realized. Trying to be understanding.

But right this minute, he just wanted to be alone.

When he looked up again, Amelia was gone. Didn't even need to walk anywhere, just vanished. He had the nerve-wracking sense that he'd done something wrong.

Time to get some sleep, then.

THE NEXT morning, one of the e-mails in the book of shadows account stood out from all the nutjobs. It caught his eye because it was articulate and full of an uncomfortable amount of detail.

"This is Amy Scanlon's book, isn't it? I assume she's dead, or you wouldn't have it. Do you know what she was, who she associated with? Have you deciphered the code yet?" Even in text, the tone seemed demanding rather than questioning, as if the sender already knew the answers to the questions.

Cormac sat back and considered. On the one hand, this sounded like someone who knew something. On the other hand, they were sure being cagey about it. Kitty's Web guru had shown him how to check for IP addresses and e-mail origins, but when he dug into the header on this one, it didn't tell him anything. The sender was using the same methods to hide his identity that Cormac used. Whoever sent this, man or woman or something else entirely, Cormac didn't trust them. Of course he didn't. But it was a thread to follow.

He wrote a reply using his own anonymous e-mail, dangling a piece of information as bait, to see what bit. "Yes, the book belonged to Amy Scanlon. She was a magician. Worked with a vampire named Kumarbis." He hit SEND and was prepared to wait for an answer, but the mail box pinged a reply after just a minute. The sender was online and ready to respond.

His blood warmed and his senses focused on the job in front of him. This was almost like hunting.

The reply read: "Where is Kumarbis?"

Dead, destroyed, but Cormac wasn't ready to say

that. He replied, "I don't know." True enough, from a certain point of view. He waited.

Another message popped up. "Who are you? You have her book—did you inherit it? Are you an apprentice of hers?"

Cormac wasn't doing a good job of fishing for information if the other guy was asking all the questions. Amy had had a checkered history; this might have been a previous teacher of hers or some other magical associate. Cormac wanted to keep him, or her, talking. "I'm a student of magic," he wrote back. "Just curious."

The reply came a moment later: "So am I."

"And who exactly are you?" Cormac sent back.

No immediate reply came, and none came after another stretch of waiting. The guy must have logged off. Or been scared off.

He shut off the laptop, sat back and considered. They'd put the book online because they wanted to see what it would dredge up. Well, here they were then. This could still be some crackpot. But the guy knew something. Maybe not how to break the code, but something. Cormac would just have to figure out how to draw him out.

LAYNE CALLED later that day, which was quicker than Cormac had expected him to.

"Cormac!" Layne said, as if they were old friends. "I pretty much figured you'd given me a fake number."

Fake numbers were too much work. "I wouldn't do that, I'm not some girl you're trying to pick up in a bar," Cormac answered.

Layne's chuckle was uncertain. "You're pretty funny."

Yeah, right. "You said you'd have something for me, Layne."

"You want to come down to my place? Talk about it in person?"

Not really, he thought. *This is the only way to learn more about Kuzniak,* Amelia reminded him. Even though this felt like walking into a bear's den in springtime.

"Sure," he said, and Layne gave him directions.

The roads to Layne's parcel of land in the hills of Fremont County weren't marked; most of them weren't even professionally built, but rather tracks that had been worn into the ground over time. The point was obvious—if you didn't get directions straight from Layne, or you didn't already know where you were going, you weren't supposed to be there. The last turn was a two-rut 4x4 trail cutting through a stand of scrub oak that opened out into a typical farmstead. An unkempt barbed wire fence, posts rotted and close to falling down, ringed the open pastureland. A post-and-wire gate could be pulled across the road, but lay off to the side for now. A square metal sign hung on the wire nearby: NO TRESPASSING it read, predictably. He drove on.

The house was a two-story clapboard box, probably a hundred years old, in decent repair. Nothing was falling off it, the roof was in one piece, and the paint wasn't too badly worn. TV dish on the roof. The barn nearby was in less good shape: unpainted, wooden sides weathered to a pale gray, roof patched with sheets of tin. The remnants of corrals marked off with rotted posts indicated the place hadn't functioned as a working ranch in a long time. A half-dozen cars and trucks, some of them covered in tarps, some of them in pieces, were parked outside the barn, along with rusted equipment—tractor frames, chain drags, and old-fashioned mowers—long ago grown over with grass and weeds.

A handful of newer, functional cars and trucks sat outside the house, and Cormac headed there, parking at the end of the row.

When he got out of the Jeep, he heard the steady pop of small arms fire on the other side of the house.

The twitch of anxiety in the back of his mind was Amelia's. *A shootout? Here?*

She still had some romantic notions about the West. This wasn't a shootout. Yes, he heard more than one gun firing—but the shots were controlled, evenly spaced out, steady. He came around to the back of the house and saw the firing range, a homemade setup, soda cans and empty beer bottles on straw bales about thirty yards out. Layne's two sidekicks from the other day were shooting semiautomatic handguns, managing to hit most of what they were aiming at. A couple of other guys, more of Layne's followers, Cormac guessed, stood by to wait their turn. Layne hung back, leaning on a fence to watch, along with Milo Kuzniak. Kuzniak was flipping the pages of a pocket-sized book, ignoring everyone else.

Knowing it would be a terrible idea to sneak up on these guys at this particular moment, he scuffed his feet on the dirt path circling the house and called a hello to Layne. One of the sidekicks still spun around, gun raised, a wild look in his eyes. Like he really was going to shoot at intruders. Cormac was expecting this and didn't even flinch. He was pretty sure that even if he did shoot, the guy was in too much of a panic to actually hit him.

You are ridiculously confident.

Smug, that's the word you're looking for.

"Roy, settle down," Layne ordered before smiling over at Cormac. The sidekicks lowered their weapons and relaxed, but only a notch. Kuzniak quickly shoved the book in a pocket. They kept eyeing Layne and each other, looking for clues about how to act. Cormac's arrival had disrupted the hierarchy. "Hey, you made it."

"Nice place," Cormac answered. "Family farm?"

"Someone else's family," Layne replied. "I got it cheap in a foreclosure a couple years ago."

Which was Layne all over, really.

"What do you need a place in the middle of nowhere for?" Cormac asked.

"Oh, this and that. Got my fingers in a lot of pies these days."

Cormac could imagine: drugs, guns, protection rackets, moonshining, scamming, general malfeasance. It's what the guy did in the bad old days, though on a much smaller scale. The barn would make a great warehouse for pot or guns. Might even have a meth lab tucked away.

He wondered if Mollie was around, and if she knew what her brother was up to. He took a look around—he remembered a couple of cars from the parking lot of the bar, but that didn't mean any of them were hers. He wasn't going to ask Layne about her.

"You want to take a turn? Get in some practice?" Layne craned his head, obviously looking for the holster Cormac wasn't wearing.

"No, I'm fine," Cormac said. There was a pause, everyone looking at him like they were waiting for an explanation. Cormac didn't give it. He nodded at Milo. "So how'd this work? Did Layne come to you because he knew something was up there, or did you go to him because you needed a backer?"

As he was sizing Milo up, Milo was sizing up him, standing apart, his gaze dark, focused—a little nerve wracking. A mousy guy like him probably worked on that stare, going for intimidation. Or he might have spent way too much time looking into other worlds. Wasn't any way to tell how much of a magician he really was until he did something. The guy didn't carry a gun, and that said something.

Cormac didn't have to work for his dark stare, not anymore. If his stare had turned otherworldly over the last few years, it probably didn't look too much different than the stone-cold stare he'd cultivated before doing time. No one would notice the difference.

"Oh, I've known Milo for a while now. He helps me with a lot of things," Layne said. "You know anything about protection spells? Charms? Sounds crazy, I know. I thought it did, 'til I saw it work."

A wizard on retainer? Was that what the criminal underworld was coming to? "Oh, I've seen a lot of crazy stuff in my day. I'm willing to give just about anything the benefit of the doubt," Cormac said.

"I figure it can't hurt to cover all my bases."

Cormac turned inward a moment, thoughtful: What do you think? Is this guy for real?

These aren't my people, Cormac. This isn't my world. I have no idea.

"I want to show you something." Layne walked off and gestured Cormac to follow him, around to the back side of the barn. Kuzniak and one of the heavies followed. So they didn't trust him, either. That was fine.

Layne pretended not to notice. "I've been having some problems. Usual kind of crap, jokers trying to edge in on my business, scare me off, whatever. Like last night, a couple of punks came through on ATVs and shot up the barn, trying to set it on fire." He pointed.

Tire tracks tore up the grass, showing how a couple of vehicles had roared in and swept around before heading back out again. Farther on, Cormac could see part of the barbed wire fence knocked over and broken. The side of the barn had scorch marks on it, streaks of soot, scars from a fire that had been quickly put out. Someone might have thrown a Molotov cocktail at the thing and had it fizzle out. The ancient, dry wood of the barn should have lit like a torch the minute flames hit it. The surrounding grass had only smoldered.

Magical protections on the property, something to quench fire or repel attack. That, or the barn had been sprayed with fire retardant. Cormac looked at Milo, who was obviously waiting for a reaction. The man quirked a smile as Cormac glanced away. Like he thought he'd won something.

Cormac ventured, "Looks like they're mostly trying to annoy you. They wanted to do damage, they'd come out here with more than a couple of bottles of gas." Cormac had to wonder what Layne had done to his would-be rivals, first.

"This is more than just a couple of kids playing tricks. This is harassment, and I know Nolan's paying them so I spend time cleaning up this shit instead of going after him."

Cormac recognized the name. Another one of the guys from the movement ten or fifteen years ago, getting back into it apparently. "Jess Nolan? You've got some gang war going on with him?"

Layne rubbed his chin and some of the bravado fell away. "Listen. I could really use your help with this. I'm holding my own, and Milo's a miracle worker. But Nolan's operation is tough—"

"Tougher than your Clanton Gang here?" Layne gave him a confused look, and Cormac shook his head, dismissing the reference.

"This is serious. They killed one of my guys last month—Roy's brother. He wasn't shot—he was torn up. I think he's got a werewolf working for them. Big guy, really tough. I shot him, I know I did, but the guy walked away like I didn't even touch him."

And that was why Layne was so happy to see a monster hunter show up. Gift from God or something. Cormac frowned. "So he's a werewolf, that's what you think? How can you tell?"

"Trust me, if you met this guy you'd know he isn't

human. I can pay you, Bennett. Take this monster out, I will pay you." He pulled a stuffed white envelope out of his jacket pocket. "Look, here—half now, half when you take care of it."

He'd been planning this out, the speech and everything.

The smart thing would be to walk away. But that was a very thick envelope. Just a few years ago, this was how Cormac made his living. Layne knew his going rate, and the envelope looked thick enough to hold just that. Time was Cormac would have considered this his duty. His calling. Now, he didn't think anything at all. He suspected Layne was wrong about this guy being a werewolf in the first place—this didn't sound like one of Kitty's pack, and they were right at the edge of her territory. She knew all the werewolves in the region. He wondered if she knew about any lone wolves out this way.

Cormac ought to just walk away, he knew he should. These people, this life—most of them ended up either in jail or dead. He didn't owe them anything. He didn't need them for anything. He should walk, even if it meant not learning a single thing more about the old Milo Kuzniak, or Amy Scanlon's book of shadows. It wasn't worth it.

But what if . . .

He couldn't tell if that was him or Amelia.

Cormac took the envelope, ran his thumb over the

hundreds inside, guessing there was about three or four thousand, and put it in his inside jacket pocket.

"I'll check it out," Cormac said. His mouth was talking but his brain hadn't quite caught up with him. "Let you know if the guy really is a werewolf and take care of it for you."

"Sounds fair."

Layne held out his hand, and Cormac shook on it.

Chapter 11

ROGUE WEREWOLF. Add another mystery to the list. He was starting to lose track.

I'm taking notes for you. Amelia's wryness made him think she was joking.

Heading back north after dusk, he stopped for gas station coffee. He had a feeling he was going to need a lot of coffee over the next few days. Jess Nolan, another blast from the past. He wondered if Ben had kept track of any of that crowd and knew what they were up to? But asking would involve telling Ben what *he* was up to.

Layne hadn't told him anything more about his operation and Cormac didn't ask, because that was how these things worked. He didn't need to know how many heavies Layne had working for him, whether they were staying in the house with him, or what their plans were. The less he knew, the better, because nobody would point to him as a witness and think he needed to be taken out—or called on to testify. Staying out of a courtroom for the rest of his life was a fine goal.

Ben complicated things when he called while Cormac was driving back north.

"You checking up on me?" Cormac said.

"Just seeing how you're doing." The casual statement was laden with subtext, a mountain of concern and curiosity.

"I got a piece of paper, that's the only thing that's changed between last week and this week."

"Funny thing how a piece of paper can make a difference. Ask me how I felt when I signed the marriage license. Humor me, Cormac—how are you?"

I might have taken on a job hunting a werewolf. . . . "I'm fine. Following up a couple of leads on this thing down in Manitou. It's gotten complicated."

"Complicated how? Anything I can do to help?"

"I'm trying to solve a hundred-year-old murder, and it looks like the guy left a few loose ends. It's just complicated. I'm fine."

"You say that enough, I may start to believe you."

He sighed. "What do you want me to say, Ben? That I'm thirty-seven years old, and since I didn't expect to live past thirty I'm not sure what to do with myself but I'm just going on the best I can?" That was more words than he usually said when he wasn't explaining something. He felt suddenly tired.

He didn't know if Ben was going to answer with something serious or flippant. He hoped flippant, because Cormac wasn't much up for serious.

"I guess that makes you just like everyone else, huh?" Ben said after a pause.

"I guess so."

A long silence while Ben waited for him to say more, when he knew very well that Cormac wasn't going to say anything.

"Be careful," Ben said finally. "Call me if I can help."

Cormac hung up.

He hit the south end of Colorado Springs and exited the interstate at Highway 24 to head into the foothills. He'd seen Kuzniak's old claim during daylight hours. Now it was time to see it at midnight. See if any ghosts came wandering out.

The moon was half full. He always knew the moon's phase, had paid close attention since he was a kid and his father started taking him hunting. His father always bought almanacs that marked the phases and circled the nights of the full moon with a thick black marker, because he almost always went hunting then. You kept track of the moon long enough, you could almost start to feel it. You always knew where to look for it, and knew if it was going to be just a smidge past full, or a sliver of new, hanging like a smile in the western sky. He still kept track, partly because it was habit and partly because of Ben and Kitty. He wanted to know when they were going out, on full moon nights.

He had a small flashlight to light his way up the path, so he wouldn't trip on rocks or tree roots. Mostly, he kept the light turned down and his gaze up, to preserve his night vision as well as he could. Moving carefully in the dark, he made slow progress. When he reached the plateau, he shut off the flashlight and put it in his pocket.

In the moonlight and nighttime shadows, the plateau looked wider, more barren. Like the scrub oak and pines were figures, creatures rising up from the ground and peering at him suspiciously.

He felt that prickling of the hairs on the back of his neck—the feeling that something odd was going on. But did it really come from something being off, or from his knowledge that something had happened here back in the day? That creeping feeling didn't provide any detail.

"You're a ghost," he said out loud. "You know any spells that find ghosts?"

Technically, I'm not a ghost. I'm merely disembodied.

He chuckled. "Semantics."

Do be polite, won't you?

"I gotta say, I wish Crane's ghost would just show up and tell us what happened." Then he could ditch

Layne, skip the werewolf hunt, and go back to just worrying about the book of shadows and Roman. Like that wasn't enough.

Crane may not have known what happened to him. It's likely he was struck dead before even realizing that his spell had failed and Kuzniak had killed him.

"Poor guy, yeah?" He kicked at a rock and kept looking over his shoulder. His breath fogged, but he didn't see anything unusual.

I have no sympathy for him, I'm afraid. He was meddling.

"Any ideas?"

I know we found signs of magic, but that just means spells were cast here. I don't think there are any ghosts, Cormac. Not of any distinct beings. Only the ghost of magic. A strong trace of magic, to last more than a hundred years.

"You'd know about that, wouldn't you?"

Indeed. If we want to know more it would be useful to have a medium here, Amelia said. *A good one whom we can trust.*

"Kitty knows one, but she's on the West Coast, I think."

Ah yes, the young lady on television. Do you suppose the people on her show would be interested in this?

"We don't have time to get them involved. We have

to keep an eye on Layne and Kuzniak before they blow something up."

Then we'd best get to work.

He arrived back in Denver around three in the morning and slept.

CORMAC DIDN'T want Ben listening in on this conversation, so he called Kitty at work. She had her radio show on Friday nights, but during the week she kept office hours at the KNOB studios, prepping for the show or cleaning up after it.

"Hey, what's up?" she answered after a couple of rings.

"You know of any lone werewolves causing trouble down south of Cañon City, around Walsenburg maybe?"

"Not since I holed up down there," she said. He could almost hear her brow furrowing as she thought about it. "I know of a couple of guys who move around the high country and the Western Slope—one of them works the ski resorts, but he's stable. He'd call me if he was having problems. That's right on the south edge of our territory, we don't go looking there very often, but I haven't heard about any problems."

This didn't surprise him. A werewolf working for a criminal element would necessarily keep a low profile.

"I've heard some rumors. Friend of a friend kind of thing."

"You think there's a rogue wolf out there? Do we need to check it out?"

He took a deep breath. "As a matter of fact, I could use your help on this."

"Of course, all you had to do was ask. I'm sure Ben can take the time—"

"Actually, I'd appreciate it if you didn't tell Ben about this."

Her tone became brusque. He smiled at the familiarity of it. "What, you think I'm not going to tell him? How am I supposed to explain my heading out to the other side of the state? 'Oh, I don't know honey, I thought I'd go shopping in La Veta for the hell of it.' "

"He's been getting kind of . . . protective."

"That's how he is. I'm not going to lie to him. And what exactly are you trying to hide from him? You didn't take a contract to hunt down this werewolf, did you?"

He couldn't come up with a sensible response to that in time for it to make a difference, so the long pause turned into an answer.

"Cormac, you *didn't,*" she declared, with a deep sense of betrayal.

"No, I didn't," he huffed, frustrated. "Not exactly."

"That's not helping!"

"This whole thing with trying to solve the mystery with Crane and Kuzniak has gotten complicated. It turns out whatever went on out there back in the day, whatever Kuzniak was doing and whatever magic those guys used up there might still be around. I've got a lead—but I've been told they've got a werewolf working for them, and I'm looking for confirmation. I just need to check it out. You feel like taking a drive?"

"You're hunting a werewolf and you want me to *help*?"

She was deliberately being thick about this, he knew that. Best thing to do was not take the bait. "Norville, every single one of my guns is still in the storage locker, and don't think I haven't noticed that Ben hasn't given me back the key. I'm just going for a drive, and I could use your help. Your opinion." Best way to handle Kitty was to appeal to her vast altruism. It was one of the most charming things about her, but it got her into trouble more often than not. He was fully aware he was getting her into trouble with this. He kept on, because he was confident she could handle it.

"Let me get this straight," she said. "You've been told there's a werewolf involved, but you don't believe it's true, and you want me to check it out. Sniff around, as it were."

"Right. Simple."

"And you want me to help, but not tell Ben, is that it?"

"I can't tell you what to do," he shot back. So yes, Ben would find out. He hoped Anderson Layne's name would stay out of it, because Ben would definitely remember Layne. Cormac would deal with that later.

"Just what exactly are you getting mixed up in?" Now she was curious.

"Nothing I can't handle."

"Some things about you haven't changed at all, you know that?"

He did. He tried not to think about it.

Chapter 12

CORMAC'S FATHER and uncle had been involved with—had gotten in trouble with—the previous heyday of the militia movement in the nineties. He shouldn't have been surprised when the whole thing started up again. He listened to the rhetoric, and it sounded the same as it ever did.

The politics of it all was irrelevant, as far as Cormac was concerned. These things moved in waves. There'd always be radicals, there'd always be discontent. The degree rose and fell, and he figured the government now wasn't any worse than the government of a hundred years ago, and mostly it was like any other bureaucracy—too big to do any good, and too ponderous to do any real evil as well. All you could do was stay out of its way, take care of you and yours. That was his real problem with most of these guys—they wanted to take care of them and theirs, and everyone else's as well. They weren't any more immune to corruption and stupidity than anyone else. And there was no worse combination than stupidity and a lot of guns.

This was the problem with these movements. They talked a big talk and their spiel sounded good, especially if you were someone who'd been screwed over by the government one too many times like a lot of these guys had been. But they ended up being a cover for bullies who saw a way to make money and get other people to take the fall for their crimes. Like Layne buying up foreclosures. Who knew what Jess Nolan was up to.

According to Layne, Nolan and his presumed werewolf held court in a bar down in Cañon City. It was a place to meet, to launder money. Likely the same function the biker bar on Highway 24 served for Layne. He picked Kitty up at the radio station, and they'd gotten all the way to southbound I-25 past Denver before either of them said anything. She was slouched in the passenger seat, head propped on her arm. Saying volumes without saying a word.

Cormac surprised himself by talking first. Kitty had successfully outwaited him. "So what did Ben say?"

"He said to make sure you stay out of trouble."

Cormac just smiled. Ben had been saying that their whole lives. And, well, Cormac was still around, wasn't he?

The drive took a couple of hours, and Kitty brought a book with her, something nonfiction about the history of Roman culture in Palestine. Research—know thine enemy, he imagined.

"Find anything good?"

"Hm?"

"In the book."

"Don't know yet. I mean, I can always learn something new. I'm just trying to figure out what he must have been like. Back before Roman became a vampire. Just curious, I guess."

She put the book away when they turned off the interstate. Cormac started looking for their destination.

"Kind of gives me the creeps, making this drive," Kitty observed. "Reminds me of coming to visit you."

Cormac did his time at one of the state prisons in Cañon City. He hadn't really thought about it until now—he'd worked to compartmentalize it, put it behind him so he could move on. But Kitty and Ben had driven here from Denver once a week for over two years to see him during visiting hours. To make sure he was okay. Kitty probably could have made this trip blindfolded. He'd never be able to show enough gratitude. He couldn't even articulate it.

"That's over and done with," he said, eyes on the road.

He found the place without too much trouble. It

was even dumpier than Layne's bar. A straight-up rectangle of a building, it might have been built in the fifties and only had spotty repairs and patching since then. The parking lot to the side might have been asphalt at one time, but the whole thing had crumbled to gravel.

Kitty stared out the Jeep's window. "My parents warned me about places like this," she said, deadpan.

"It probably looks scarier than it is."

"Does anything ever look scary to you?"

Prison ceilings at night. The door to solitary confinement. The thought of calling Ben and Kitty and them not answering.

Death . . .

That, not so much.

He got out, slammed the door. Back in the day, he'd have worn a handgun in a belt holster, more for credibility than out of any intention to use it. He wondered if he'd ever get used to not carrying a gun, or if he'd always feel a little too light. Like he'd lost a limb or something.

Kitty climbed out of the Jeep more slowly, regarding the building with increasing skepticism as she shut the door.

She said, "If there's really a werewolf here, he probably considers this his territory, and he'll notice me before we notice him."

He'd thought of that. He wasn't worried. "If that's

the case, he'll give you a warning, tell you to leave—and we'll know what we came to find out."

"That's the best-case scenario. He may not bother with the warning."

"I'm sure you can talk it out," he said.

Arms loose at her side, she walked across the parking lot, moving parallel to the building rather than heading for the door. She studied the area, and her nose was working—chin tipped up, nostrils wide, her breaths coming slow. He stopped to watch her.

"I'm not smelling anything," she said after a couple of minutes.

If a werewolf had even just walked across the parking lot at any point in the last few days, she'd have sensed it. If one regularly spent time here, she'd definitely smell it. That seemed to be his answer right there. But he had to be sure.

"Right," he said. "Let's go in."

"I want to go on record as saying that this makes me nervous."

"We'll go in, sit down, have a drink, and leave. It'll be fine. I'll buy."

"Well, how can a girl refuse an offer like that?"

The inside was marginally better looking than the outside. The linoleum floor seemed to be from the eighties rather than the fifties, at least. The wooden tables and chairs were mismatched, as if they'd been acquired at thrift stores over the last couple of decades. The lighting was appropriately dim. There were people here, a sparse collection of working-class-looking men sitting at the bar and at a couple of tables—coming off shift, or working irregular jobs. A worn-out woman in her forties was both bartender and waitress. She spotted Cormac and Kitty as they came in and told them to sit anywhere, she'd be right over.

"Would you know this guy if you saw him?" Kitty asked.

"I'd probably recognize Nolan. This guy who's supposed to be a werewolf, I don't know who he is."

"He's not a werewolf. I'd smell him. My Wolf would smell him. Who told you he was a werewolf?"

"Somebody's spreading stories. Intimidating people, convincing people he uses magic. I think it's all a put-on. I was told this guy killed somebody by tearing him to pieces. Hence, werewolf."

"A dead body can be made to look as if it was torn to pieces. There're other things than werewolves that tear bodies to pieces."

"Well, something's going on. I want to know what."

The waitress came by and they ordered Cokes. Cormac stopped her before she turned away. "Do you know a guy named Jess Nolan? Heard he comes in here sometimes. I'm an old friend."

"Yeah, sure, I know Jess. He usually shows up late. Want me to tell him you stopped by?"

"No, that's okay, I'll track him down."

Some of the guys in the place looked over, studied him a second, and looked away. Cormac pretended not to notice, but at this point he half expected them all to be familiar faces from the old days. Guys who knew his uncle, his dad, and would saunter on up to him wanting to know if he still killed werewolves. All these old faces, all this talk that was like a scab breaking off.

"How many of these guys have guns on 'em?" he asked Kitty softly.

She tilted her head, half closed her eyes. The wolfish gestures took over, as she studied the air the way he might have studied the room's layout. But the wince and furrowed brow was all human. "All of them? Or a couple of them have more than one."

"Right." He drank most of the Coke, pulled a five out of the inside pocket of his jacket and threw it on the table as he stood to leave.

"So that's it?" Kitty added a couple of bucks of her own—a conscientious tip—before joining him on the way to the door.

"One other place I want to check out." Some of the old haunts might very well turn up something. Even though part of him was saying he should walk away. This was trouble, and he was supposed to be keeping his nose clean.

Just looking can't hurt.

Famous last words, he muttered back.

They got back on the road, traveling west until he turned down yet another county road, rural and unmarked, lined with barbed wire and cattle crossing signs. Graded gravel kicked up to rattle the side of the Jeep. This road wound into the foothills. He was looking for a shed at an abandoned mine. Some friends of his uncle used it to store their stockpile back in the day. He didn't remember hearing that the Feds had ever cleared this one out, and he had a hunch if anyone in the area was still keeping it up, it might be Nolan.

"Where the hell are we?" Kitty observed, leaning forward to search out the window. "I haven't been down in this part of the state in *years*."

"How much has Ben told you about the shit his dad was into?"

"Not much. He doesn't like to talk about it. Most of what I know I picked up from the newspaper articles I dug up. He was some kind of bigwig in the local militia movement. His conviction was for illegal weapons stockpiling and conspiracy, some kind of plan to set off a bomb at the state capitol from what I gathered. Didn't get very far."

"That's because the Feds had so much surveillance on him by then they knew when he brushed his teeth. They waited long enough for him to actually say the plan out loud so they could get the charges on him.

But there's a lot that didn't make the papers. Not about Uncle David specifically—I think he really believed in what he was doing, but Ben would rather write him off as crazy. Some of those other guys, though—you have to ask how they got the money to buy all those weapons. They like to take capitalism as far as they can, you know? Illegal doesn't matter as long as they make money off it."

"What, so they were bank robbers? Smugglers? Drug dealers?"

"All of the above? Yeah. So, that's what I think Layne and Nolan are into. Last few years, what with the economy tanking and the last election, the movement's been making a comeback, getting popular again. Guys like that'll use the whole thing as a cover and a recruiting ground."

"Can we go home now?" she said. She had a sour look on her face. She'd been gripping the door handle for the last five miles as the Jeep bounced over barely-there roads.

"Just half an hour."

"What does Amelia say about all this?"

"She says it can't hurt to look."

"No, I mean about the militia stuff. Your family."

He turned inward a moment and got nothing articulate. Just the quiet watchfulness she had when he was immersed in modernity.

"Says it's not her world," he answered and left it at that.

"Someday I'm going to talk you both into letting me interview her on the show."

I believe that would be a bad idea. Cormac agreed, and if Kitty hadn't talked them into it by now, she never would.

"There it is," he said, steering the Jeep around a curve and to a turnout. The place would be just around the next hill.

As he left the Jeep, he put his hand in his pocket, keeping hold of a bit of sage and the lighter, more to steady himself than any thought that he'd be able to use it. If they ran into trouble, there'd be guns, and Amelia didn't know any spells to protect against that. They'd either have to run for it or talk their way out of it.

One step at a time.

Kitty moved ahead, her nose tipped into the air, flaring. When she glanced back at him, she looked worried. "I don't like this."

He steered her on, over a rise and into a dip between hills, not quite big enough to be a valley. Treeless, gravelly earth sloped downward to a weather-worn, unpainted shed. He didn't see anyone, but Kitty was right, something was off here. Like a roomful of people holding their breath.

Back in the day, the shed hid the entrance to the abandoned mine tunnel where the weapons stockpile was kept. Now, the whole thing looked deserted. That was probably the idea.

"Cormac, something's wrong here," Kitty said. She'd gone into full danger stance, her shoulders bunched up and her back hunched, like hackles rising. Her arms hung at her sides, her fingers curled into claws. She stopped, knees bent, like she expected to have to run.

"What do you smell?"

"That's just it, it's not a smell, it's a feeling, it's just *wrong*. Dead, rotten, evil—Cormac, I remember this, from back in Walsenberg—" Her shocked eyes and the edge of panic in her voice triggered his own memories.

"Skinwalker," he said. "Shit."

Right pocket, arrowhead charm.

He took out the arrowhead, tied to a simple leather cord, and pulled it down around his neck. It said something, that he didn't remember half the stuff Amelia had had him keep in his pockets. The Navajo arrowhead was a simple enough charm, but promised sure protection against skinwalkers: shape-shifters, but not lycanthropes. It was a very dark kind of magic. A skinwalker was a specific type of Navajo magician, required to perform human sacrifice in exchange for their powers. The last skinwalker Cormac encountered was a woman. Killing her, even in defense, had sent him to prison. Something about "excessive force . . ."

So, Nolan didn't have a werewolf working with him. He had one of these bastards.

He was about to tell Kitty to get back in the Jeep when the wolf came at her, crashing through the pine trees at the edge of the clearing and charging. Her, not him—maybe it could tell what she was and identified her as the bigger threat. Or maybe the arrowhead charm actually worked. Whatever it was, the wolf slammed into her, jaw open and angled for her neck. She didn't have time to run.

He'd never missed the presence of a gun in his hand more than he did now. But right now, even if he had a gun, he wouldn't have been able to shoot because they were tangled up together—no way to get a clear target on the other wolf, the skinwalker.

Kitty looked thin and willowy and blond and breakable, but she'd been in scrapes before and was stronger than she seemed. Curling her own lips to show teeth, she let the wolf knock her over, then kept rolling to get herself on top. She went for eyes and groin, tearing with bent fingers that were suddenly looking longer, sharper than human.

The thing was dark, hulking, snarling, and its eyes glowed an otherworldly, gemlike red. It didn't have any of the grace or power of a natural wolf, or even an oversized lycanthropic variety. It was a bundle of hate and wrongness, biting and slashing. Kitty was holding her own, mostly because her supernatural speed and agility allowed her to duck and dodge. She was strong enough to knock the other wolf back once or twice, to get in a few hits. But she couldn't do much else, not as a human.

Cormac ran to the back of the Jeep and to the emergency kit he kept there. Digging around, he found the pair of roadside flares stashed in it. Ran back to the fight.

The beast slashed and snapped at Kitty; a flash of red sprayed—that was Kitty's blood. She was using her arms to block, and they were taking damage. Both were snarling, growling. He couldn't tell which noises were coming from whom.

Holding the flares in one hand, he lit them with his lighter. Even in daylight they glowed red and threw off sparks. Holding them aloft, he stalked toward the fight, making himself as big and threatening as he could, hoping to scare off the attacker. He swung his arms, making arcs of smoke and fire.

It worked. The skinwalker kicked and writhed to get out from under Kitty—opening more scratches, but Kitty didn't seem to notice. As it scrambled into the open, it turned and ran, back stiff and tail straight out like a rudder. A werewolf would have had its tail tucked between its legs, getting driven off after a fight like that. But a skinwalker was a human in wolf skin, not a being made up of parts of both.

"Kitty?" he called at her.

Crouching, she stared out into the woods, growling with every breath, an amber sheen in her eyes. Her T-shirt was ripped and hanging off her, revealing skin and bra. She'd torn it off herself, and was now shoving down her jeans. Her teeth were long, and her face was stretching.

"Kitty," he repeated warningly, even as he backed away to give her room. Her wolf half would recognize him. At least, it had before.

"Gotta track down that bastard," she muttered, her voice thick.

"No, you don't—"

She was already shifting. Adrenaline and blood had pushed her wolfish instincts over the edge. Even as she stripped, a sheen of gray and tawny fur sprouted over her naked skin as her limbs seemed to melt, twisting into new shapes. She grunted once in pain, but other than that the change seemed to flow through her, like she'd flipped a switch and let it happen. He looked away, unable to face full-on the sight of her caught between one shape and another, her form distorted.

Then it was over, and an oversized wolf—long, rangy legs, lean body, pointed ears focused forward—was shaking off the last of her clothes. Without looking back she launched into a ground-eating run, chasing the skinwalker into the woods. She might very well be even more pissed off at the thing than he was.

When shots fired—explosive punctuation to the already chaotic encounter—Cormac crouched to take himself out of any line of fire. Looking, he found a man some thirty yards off, near the worn-out shed, aiming a rifle in the direction Kitty's wolf had raced off.

Chapter 13

FURY GRABBED Cormac, with an urge to race over, yank the rifle out of the guy's hands and beat him over the head with it until his skull caved in. Then keep going. He didn't do that, because that was likely to get him shot. A quick assessment—the shots hadn't gotten her. Kitty was still running, quickly disappearing into the trees. The gunman kept shooting anyway, wasting bullets.

Ben was going to kill him for getting her into this.

How were we supposed to know it was a skinwalker, not a werewolf? My God. Even Amelia sounded breathless.

Cormac wasn't so sure Ben would understand. If the roles had been reversed, he'd be inclined to break the other's neck for putting Kitty in danger. Kitty wouldn't even be able to stop him. Fortunately, Ben was a lot more rational than that. He'd at least wait for an explanation. He might not ever talk to Cormac again after, but he'd listen to the excuses first.

In the end, he recognized the gunman, which kept Cormac from murdering the guy straight off. Thickset, bearded, in a green canvas jacket and faded jeans. Jess Nolan, of course. Cormac tipped his head back, looking heavenward in a vague prayer, then stood, held up his arms and the flares in a show of peace, and called out. "Hey!"

His eyes buggy with shock, Nolan swung the rifle around, but lowered it when he saw Cormac. He squinted like he didn't believe what he was seeing.

"Bennett? Cormac Bennett, is that you?"

Cormac hadn't thought he was famous until the last few days. He'd had a reputation years ago, but he figured it wouldn't have survived his time in prison plus a couple of years of mostly staying out of trouble. Oh well.

"Jess Nolan," he said by way of reply. A statement as well as an expression of annoyance.

Nolan's laugh was nervous, like he was pretending to be happy to see him, and trying to ignore what had just happened. Tucking the rifle under his arm, he came over, holding his hand out like he expected Cormac to shake it. Cormac had his hands full of road flare and didn't move.

"What are you doing out here, Bennett?" He tried to sound casual, but kept looking back into the trees.

Trying to decide which was the bigger threat, Cormac or the werewolf he'd just seen go tearing off.

Cormac took a pointed look at the torn grass and bloodied ground where the fight had taken place, as well as the abandoned-looking shed and mine entrance. "Just out for a walk with a friend. You're a little jumpy with that gun, you think?"

His nervous smile dropped. "Friend—you don't mean that wolf?"

"I do. I figure that's why you're out here—just you and a wolf, out for a walk?"

"Sure. I guess." He was standing between Cormac and the shed. Guarding it.

"You want to tell me about the skinwalker?"

"The what?" he said flatly. Cormac wasn't buying the dumb act.

"You've got some jumpy Navajo wizard working for you patrolling the place, right? Maybe getting in fights?"

"How do you know about that shit?"

Cormac gave him a look; his patience was gone. "I'm not interested in your stash, Nolan. I'm going to go track my friend down now, and I'd appreciate it if you called off your buddy before she gets to him." And so Cormac didn't have to keep looking over his shoulder.

"Your friend? A *werewolf.* I thought you hunted down werewolves."

Yeah, so did he. His father's memory chastised him yet again. "Yeah, well, there was this girl. What the hell you doing out here that you need muscle like that? What is it Layne thinks you're doing out here?"

"*Layne* sent you?"

"I'm out here on my own, but yeah, I've talked to him, and I want to know what the hell's got the two of you so worked up."

"Layne's crazy," Nolan said. "Paranoid. I'm trying to stay out of his way, but he keeps thinking I'm moving in on him, but I'm not, I swear. I mean, I might have hassled him a little, but that's it. You go tell him I'm not moving in."

"He thinks you have a werewolf working for you."

"No, that's just Eddie."

Eddie the skinwalker. Shit. "So, you still keeping a stash out here? Is that it? What are you planning on doing with it?"

Flustered now, Nolan looked like he was thinking of denying it. But then he shook his head. His hands might have been shaking. "You're right, I'm keeping the stash up, and Eddie's helping me keep an eye on the place. I got a right to it. You can't have it back."

"I don't want it back. You keep it. Shit, have fun with it."

"Trust me, when the Feds come around to take everyone's guns, I'll have the fallback. I'll sell the whole thing off on the black market and make an absolute shit-ton of money."

"Yeah, you and the thousand other guys in the state who are thinking the same thing." Cormac was just pushing the guy's buttons now. Hard to resist—he kept getting redder.

"Why aren't you carrying?" Nolan shot back. "You gone soft?"

"Naw, I just got tired of people mistaking me for someone like you."

Nolan raised the rifle again with rigid arms, stiff hands, and a furious glare. Even as close as he was, the guy was angry enough to miss Cormac if he actually fired. But Cormac put up his arms again and tried not to smirk too hard.

"Take it easy," Cormac said. "I'm not here for you or your stash, I just came to see if anyone was still out here. I'll be glad to leave just as soon as I track down my friend. You want to maybe help me out, maybe try to find your guy before he gets torn up?"

"There's no way anything can hurt Eddie, not when he's all wolfed out like that."

"You ever actually meet a real-live werewolf? Or just Eddie's version of one?" He didn't answer, which meant no. "Let's go save your friend's ass."

Turning his back on Nolan and his rifle, he found a bare spot of dirt to set the flares on until they burned out, then gathered up Kitty's clothes, torn and probably useless as they were, to set them on the Jeep's passenger seat for when she came back. Pulled the blanket out of his emergency kit, along with a canteen of water, and started walking. Footsteps crunching on gravel indicated Nolan was following.

Truth was, he didn't think Kitty would actually kill the guy. She was certainly capable of it, but right now, she was angry, not homicidal.

"Bennett, what are you doing hanging out with a werewolf?" Nolan, still trailing, demanded. Cormac didn't feel the need to answer. "I know your rep, your dad's rep. You *kill* werewolves."

Cormac ignored him.

The two wolves left a clear trail, tearing through underbrush and kicking up soil. Nolan was muttering the whole time and Cormac almost told him to shut up so he could listen for the wolves up ahead. Then he figured, why bother? Kitty wasn't going to stop and wait. Eventually, she'd have to bed down, and that was when he'd be likely to find her. His goal was to keep the skinwalker away from her when she did. He'd need Nolan for that.

"You never told me how you got mixed up with a skinwalker," Cormac prompted, looking over his shoulder at the lagging Nolan.

"Nothing to tell. We're just a couple guys with a business."

"He's Navajo?"

"Half Navajo—how'd you know that, you haven't even seen him. I mean, not *really* seen him, as a human."

"Just knew it." Really, half of the trick to seeming omniscient was paying attention.

"So are you back in the business? You disappeared for a while there—a couple of the guys thought you were dead, you know? But if somebody really was having a werewolf problem—"

"No," he said. "I'm not back in the business."

He heard something up ahead and held out his arm to get Nolan to stop and be quiet. It was snarling, the tearing of underbrush in a scuffle. He crept forward as if he were hunting, watching for that flash of movement.

With her supernatural strength and animal instincts, Kitty had overtaken the skinwalker, forcing him to engage her in a crowded stand of pines. The two animals circled, taking swipes at each other and dodging. Kitty was easy to spot—pure wolf, her muzzle wrinkled back to show a snout full of teeth, ears flat to her head, hackles making her appear twice as large. The other one—he snarled, snapped, growled, showed teeth, and sprang out of reach of Kitty's claws easy enough. But he wasn't a wolf. His tail was loose, its position undetermined, his ears were up like radar dishes, and he bounced like a dog. His red eyes were visible as glowing points.

The skinwalker had managed to keep out of her way this long, but unless he got lucky, she'd eventually pin him. Cormac had no idea if the guy's magic would protect him from the bite of a werewolf, but he was pretty sure Kitty wouldn't want to find out. She'd feel responsible for the guy if she infected him. Cormac would just as soon she killed the bastard.

"Kitty!" he called.

Nolan stared at him. "Its name is *Kitty*?"

Cormac just glared. Her ears came up for a split second, but she never let her attention waver from her enemy. "Kitty, we got this, back the hell off!"

Nolan took the cue. "Eddie! Get out of there! Just leave it!"

The growling dropped off; the two creatures put a fraction more space between them. But they continued circling, heads down and muscles tensed.

"I'm not breaking up that fight," Nolan declared.

Cormac's hand itched for a gun. He could fire it into the woods to get their attention. Kitty wasn't going to break off until the other wolf showed some sign of submission. But he wasn't really a wolf, and so it wasn't likely to happen.

"Nolan, tell him to drop his gaze and his tail."

"What?"

"He needs to break eye contact, get his tail down so she'll leave him alone. Do it!"

"Eddie! You heard him. He knows what he's talking about, do what he says, okay?"

The scraggly wolf turned and looked at Nolan, and Cormac swore he could read the animal's expression: What, seriously? Disbelief and frustration. But he gave a shake, dropped his gaze, and let his tail fall. If not a show of submission, it at least said that he wasn't going to put up any more fight.

In response, Kitty backed up a step. Her gaze fell, her tail relaxed. Her fur was still sticking straight up—she wasn't going to trust the guy if she could help it. The standoff continued, since neither one of them was going to walk away.

"Kitty, it's okay. I got this." Her ear flicked, but otherwise she didn't move. "Go sleep it off. Please," he said.

She dropped her head, paced in a circle a couple of times, looking them all over as if trying to make a decision. Finally, she loped off, weaving between trees, down a rise, and out of sight, looking at home in the forest, as natural as breathing. He sighed, frustrated at how politeness always seemed to work on her, even in her wolf form, like she was some kind of schoolteacher.

Nolan let out a heavy breath he'd been holding. "Jesus Christ, I thought we were all dead."

Which showed he didn't know anything about

werewolves. Her posture had been angry, but defensive. In the meantime, the other wolf seemed to hunch its shoulders, cocking its head, wriggling itself into a seated position, propped up on its hind legs. Then, a human hand reached out from under the mass of fur, grabbed hold of a now-lifeless tuft of skin near its neck, and pulled. Cormac had confronted skinwalkers before, but he'd never seen one shift back to human like this.

The skin came off, and a twenty-something man, naked, stood tall in the wolf's place, holding the wolf hide in front of him to shield his privates. He had deeply tanned skin, short black hair, and a lopsided grin, like he was waiting for someone to laugh at his joke.

Nolan cleared this throat. "Uh, Bennett? This is Eddie. Eddie, Cormac Bennett."

Cormac said, "You know, I don't care who the hell you are or what the hell you're getting up to out here. I'm gonna go after my friend, hike back to my Jeep, and leave you to it."

He turned to march off, but Eddie moved to intercept him. Not saying a word, not caring that he was stark naked except for a mangy-looking, tattered wolf skin. He still had a predator's look in his eye, like he was waiting for a chance to pounce.

So it was going to go like this, was it?

Nolan said, "First, you tell me when Layne's planning on moving in. You say he didn't send you, but why else would you be out here?"

"You'll have to ask him," Cormac said, again making to step around Eddie, who again moved to block. This was going to get old real quick. He looked the guy straight on, meeting his gaze. "Who'd you kill to get this power?"

The guy's smile turned toothy. "Huh. Smart guy, are you?"

Cormac tugged at the arrowhead charm to make sure it showed over his T-shirt. "Move."

Eddie didn't move. But he wasn't smiling anymore. Cormac's awareness had gone sharp, his skin prickling and the air going still, the way it did before a fight or at the critical moment of a hunt, right before he fired a shot. Eddie was in front of him, unhappy but unable to do anything because the charm worked. Out of the corner of his eye, he saw Nolan moving up behind him, but his rifle was tucked under his arm, hanging at his side. He was complacent, because he had Eddie to do his dirty work.

At least they weren't going after Kitty.

"Eddie, you going to lay this fucker out or what?" he said. Probably not as casually as he wanted. All he had to do was take another step closer . . .

"Can't," Eddie said. "He's protected."

"What?"

"Because I know what I'm doing," Cormac said,

and dropped his gear to swing back into Nolan with an elbow in the solar plexus. He followed with a right hook that made the guy stumble and drop the rifle entirely. Then Nolan surprised him by taking a swing back. He didn't seem capable. Cormac dodged, but the blow caught him on the cheek, rattled his head. Didn't matter, he ignored it and grabbed Nolan's shirt, threw him to the ground, and kicked him in the gut, just to get it over with. The whole time, Eddie didn't make a move. He frowned, though, shuddering in place like he desperately wanted to go for blood.

Nolan writhed a moment, letting loose a collection of the usual curses while pawing around for his dropped weapon. As tempting as it would be to also kick the man in the groin while he was down, Cormac resisted. He found the rifle, popped open the chamber and unloaded it, scattering the bullets into the underbrush and throwing away the weapon. He collected the blanket and canteen and set off. This time, Eddie didn't move to block his way.

He was maybe thirty feet away when Nolan found the rifle, grabbed extra bullets from his pocket, loaded it, and collected himself enough to be able to aim, Cormac saw when he glanced over his shoulder. He kept walking. The shot never came.

Cormac turned, walking back a few steps as he called, "What, you too chicken to shoot?"

Nolan snarled and called back, "You ain't worth the bullet!"

Well, that was something.

After that, Eddie and Nolan had some kind of argument, Cormac couldn't hear about what. They stalked off—and not in the direction of the shed. They must have had a car parked somewhere. A car and a mission. He wondered if he ought to call Layne, give him a heads-up.

You are going to have to watch your back.

Sure, but no more so than usual. The fact that Eddie couldn't touch him had freaked Nolan out—the guy didn't know what else Cormac could do and wasn't going to take a chance on provoking him. If he tried to retaliate by, say, slashing the Jeep's tires, Cormac might come back and magically blow up the whole site. Never mind whether or not he actually could.

Why do people make things so difficult?

The thing was, you just had to make sure you had a way to carve a path right through other people's difficulties.

So glad we're having success with that lately.

Ghosts—or disembodied spirits—shouldn't be allowed to use sarcasm.

Chapter 14

WALKING AWAY, Cormac's cheek started to hurt. Probably meant that Nolan's hand hurt worse, so that was all right.

Kitty's wolf barely left a trail when she wasn't racing. The creature stepped lightly, displacing only a paw-print's worth of dirt every now and then. But he had a good idea what direction she'd gone, and she seemed to keep a straight path. He searched for an hour, which was fine because that gave her enough time to find a place to bed down and fall asleep in order to make the shift back to human.

He found her, a lean stretch of pale skin in contrast to the surrounding brown underbrush. She was curled up in fetal position, knees pulled to her chest and arms bent close to her body, head tucked in. He could see the shape of the wolf that had fallen asleep like that, limbs pulled in tight, tail tucked across nose. Now, she was human, naked, her blond hair a tangle blending into the strewn leaves around her. She was tense, her brow furrowed, as if she was caught in a bad dream.

He'd intended to sit back and wait for her to wake up in her own time. Picking a spot a little ways off, he sat on the ground against a tree trunk. That only lasted a minute. It was voyeuristic, kinky almost, him watching her sleep. Obviously, she'd had enough time to shift back, whether or not she was fully rested. They ought to get a move on.

"Hey. Kitty."

She jerked, coming to awareness and instantly propping herself up to look around with wide, startled eyes.

"Whoa." She slumped over, shook her head, stretched. He looked away. "Fucking skinwalker, who'd have thunk? Who was that guy?"

He sidled over, holding out the blanket as he continued to look off in the distance, though he could see her in the corner of his vision. He tried not to.

"Backwoods yahoo. Hired muscle. He won't bother us again." She seemed totally unselfconscious. Why should she be, she was a werewolf.

"Thanks," she murmured, taking the blanket and wrapping it around herself. "Sorry about that. I probably shouldn't have run off, but it was the only way we were going to track him."

"Let's just get the hell out of here."

"But he's dangerous—what if he comes after us?"

"We had a talk. He's one of Nolan's guys. Their whole operation up here is high school shit, not worth messing with." Maybe he did kill Roy's brother in some scuffle, or maybe that was all just a story. One way or the other, Cormac wasn't about to get wrapped up in this mess.

"If you say so. Thanks for the blanket." She climbed to her feet and rearranged the blanket for the trip through the woods, revealing glimpses of skin. Not that Cormac was looking.

She peered at him. "You know you have the start of a really pretty black eye?" She started to reach out to touch it, but winced and pulled away.

"It's just a bruise. Zigged when I should have zagged."

"Should we be grateful you weren't shot?"

"Probably." He walked on, and she followed.

"This may all be high school shit to you, but they've got guns and bad intentions and you're getting involved." She waited; he didn't say anything, because what was there to say? "Just promise me you're not getting sucked into anything that's going to get you in trouble. I never want to have to make that drive to Cañon City again."

He glanced at her and had to smile because she looked ridiculous, her hair hanging in tangles around her face, the gray blanket slipping off her shoulders as she clung to it. He had that wrenching feeling again, a flashback to when he'd intended to kill her, when she was just another job. And then—that endearing look that she was turning to him right now. The optimism. She trusted him, and that seemed the weirdest part of all. Any other ache he felt was superfluous. Old news.

"I promise," he said.

"Good."

WHEN THEY got back to the shed, Nolan and Eddie were both gone, which was good. It saved Cormac from having to do any more posturing. Who knew how much kerosene he'd already poured on the whole mess just by coming down here and mentioning Layne to Nolan. The war between them might have all been in Layne's head—was it still?

He ought to just walk away.

Back at the Jeep, Kitty dressed as best she could, scowled at her torn shirt but managed to fit it on anyway, but held on to the blanket. Cormac kept busy retrieving the burnt-out flares and checking over the Jeep. The tires were intact, and it hadn't acquired any new dents or scratches.

Nolan probably had a single-wide or some cabin out here or at the edge of town. Scraping by at the edges. Eddie might have been crashing at his place, might have had a dump of his own. Cormac didn't much care. They'd be back here soon—he wouldn't have scared them off entirely and probably didn't have more than ten or fifteen minutes to check out the shed. But he wanted to check it out. He retrieved his gloves and flashlight out of the front of the Jeep.

"Wait here a second," he said to Kitty.

"What? What are you doing?" she asked as he walked off.

"Just wait."

She growled, slumping against the Jeep's hood and crossing her arms to keep her shirt on.

What are you planning? Amelia, also checking up on him. He was getting it from both sides now. Typical.

"Those two'll be back after us if I don't take care of them," Cormac said.

That doesn't answer my question.

"You'll see."

Of course I will. Bloody hell.

Flashlight in hand, he went through the shed and into the mouth of the tunnel, a symmetrical opening of granite, roughhewn with nineteenth-century tools and smelling of chalk. The place hadn't changed much. The same chain-link gate was bolted across the tunnel a few feet in. The metal NO TRESPASSING sign had been replaced with a plastic one at some point. So had the padlock, a straightforward commercial one with a key, which Cormac set about picking and had open in under a minute.

The tunnel on the other side of the door didn't go too far back; the rest of the place had collapsed and filled in with debris years ago. It wasn't below the water table, which meant the extant cave stayed cool and dry—not a bad place to store a weapons cache. And there it was, crates stacked up, metal gun lockers shoved against stone walls, cheap metal shelving holding boxes of ammunition. Further back he found some other survivalist gear—boxes of canned and dried food, army surplus MREs, blankets, bottled water, batteries, radios. A nice little setup. All on federal land, which was a problem if Nolan didn't have someone in the Forest Service covering for him, the way Uncle David had back in the day. He wondered.

Part of him had an urge to strike up his lighter in here. Find a fuse, light it all up, watch it go boom. That'd piss more than a few people off.

But he didn't see much sense in setting the whole valley on fire. He ignored the itching in his hand and walked back out. After replacing the lock on the gate, he emerged into warm sunshine.

"Well?" Kitty asked when he got back to the Jeep.

"Well what?"

"I figured you went off to blow something up," she said.

Was he really that predictable? "I have a better idea," he said. "You'll like this one."

She seemed skeptical, studying him with a raised brow. He wrote down the GPS coordinates of the spot, then they drove down the mountain for better cell reception.

Guys like Nolan and Layne would call what he was about to do ratting out. They'd call him a snitch and a bastard with as much contempt as they knew how to muster. What Cormac figured: wasn't much point holding to some kind of honor system where folk like Nolan and Layne were concerned. Cormac had a goal, and that was to get Nolan and his crew out of the way so he didn't have to worry about them. If he had an easy way to do it without implicating himself in anything that might get him thrown back in prison? All the better.

Pulling over, he called information and got the number for the San Isabel National Forest district office. As he was hoping, he got a menu that let him leave a message rather than talking to someone. They'd see his phone number, but he wouldn't have to talk to them if he didn't want to.

He could sound like an upstanding citizen when he needed to, pitching his voice just a little higher and sounding a little bit confused. "Hi, yeah, I was hiking up south of Cotopaxi on one of the service roads and

I found something weird. Didn't look right, and I don't know who to tell, but I figured you all would want to know. Looks like someone's got a storage locker or something in one of the old caves up there. It's locked up. A lot of bullet casings on the ground, stuff like that. I thought maybe it might be drugs or something; I didn't really want to stick around, just in case. But I thought you guys would want to know. I had my GPS with me." He listed off the coordinates and ended the call without giving his name.

Now he just had to wait and see what happened.

Kitty was staring at him. Ignoring her, he pulled back onto the road, heading for the highway and the long drive home.

"The indirect approach? *You?*" she said finally.

"I might as well let someone else do the work for me."

Shaking her head, she giggled. "I am constantly in awe of how sneaky you can be."

Wasn't trying to be sneaky. He just had a job and wanted to get it done with as little fuss as possible.

She slept on the drive back to Denver, which told him he hadn't let her sleep long enough back in the woods and she was still recovering from shifting. Weird, to feel so protective. Of a werewolf. He'd never get over the disconnect.

Could have been so much different if he'd been

able to, when he first met her. Years ago now, but he still thought of it. Maybe it should have been different.

Amelia sounded put out when she muttered at him. *I know what happened. You showed me what happened, letting it seep out of your memories whether you liked it or not. You had your chance with her. She gave you a chance, and you walked away. Can you imagine what that does to a woman? She's told all her life that what men want is carnal knowledge of her, she offers herself, her body to you—and you refuse her? All she can think is, My God, what is wrong with me?*

"She's a werewolf." That was his excuse. He'd gotten close—sometimes he imagined he could still taste her lips, feel her eager hands gripping him. Then some kind of flight instinct kicked in. Self-preservation, and suddenly he could only see that he was feeding himself to the wolf. He'd gotten scared. *Him,* scared.

He still saw the wolf in her. He just didn't mind it so much, now.

At least you have the sense to accept her friendship.

Glad you approve, he muttered back.

I'm only trying to be helpful.

KITTY'S PHONE—sitting on the edge of the seat, tucked against her leg where she'd set it before she fell asleep—rang a couple of times before Cormac took the liberty of shutting it off. Ben, both times. Cormac didn't want to talk to Ben. He probably should have woken her up so she could deal with it, but he didn't. Dodging. He shut the thing off so she wouldn't hear the ringing.

Dusk had fallen when they finally pulled into the driveway of her house. Ben kept odd hours and was often out, meeting with clients, springing them from jail, or jumping through hoops at court. Cormac was hoping that Ben would be out when he dropped Kitty off.

She was awake by then, wrapped up in the blanket. The slashes on her arms from the skinwalker had healed, but he was pretty sure traces of blood still lingered in her clothing and that Ben would smell it. Not to mention the lopsided shiner he'd developed, a purplish half moon sloping under his left eye. He kept poking at the puffy skin, and yeah, it hurt. He ought to get some ice on it. He didn't want to have to explain any of it to his cousin. His plan was to let her out without him ever getting out of the car. She could do all the talking. She was good at it.

But Ben was waiting in the driveway. He must have heard the Jeep's engine and come out to meet them. He was barefoot, in his casual/sloppy mode, wearing jeans and an untucked T-shirt, and his arms were crossed.

Kitty scrambled for her phone. "Why is it off? Did you turn it off?" She fiddled with it a few seconds and groaned. "He's been trying to call for an hour. Did you turn your phone off, too?"

"Yup."

She let out a growl and stormed out of the car, slamming the door behind her.

He still might have had a chance to escape, but Ben came over and put a hand on the roof over the driver's-side door. Cormac had spent all day going face-to-face with blowhards, and found he couldn't stand up to Ben. He rolled down the window.

Kitty went around and leaned next to her husband.

"And how was your day?" Ben asked wryly.

She said, "You're gonna have to ask him, I'm done playing go-between."

Ben tilted his head, took a searching breath. "You shifted. What happened—wait a minute, are you *bleeding*?" The anger vanished. He held her shoulders, faced her, studied her all over, searching and smelling.

"Not anymore," she said brightly.

He breathed a word that might have been a curse, wrapped his arm around her shoulders and pulled her into an embrace, kissing her forehead, resting there a moment. When he turned back to yell at Cormac, he didn't let her go. Kept that arm around her, kept her pulled close, and she melted into the contact.

Cormac thought, not for the first time, that she was better off with him. He couldn't do what Ben did, wrapping her up with affection so casually. She got sliced up and the best Cormac could do to comfort her was hand her a blanket.

Ben said, "What the *hell* have you gotten into? And is that a black eye? You got into a fight? Thank God you're off parole."

He didn't know where to start, and when he looked at Kitty—the talker, who was so much better at explaining things than he was—she wasn't any help. She blinked those big brown eyes expectantly at him and stayed quiet.

Cormac sighed. "You remember Anderson Layne?"

He had to think about it a minute. Kitty was watching for his reaction. "The militia nut who hung out with my dad? You ran into him? While looking into a century-old murder? I'm confused."

"I didn't go looking for him. He's hired himself a wizard and is getting into the prospecting business. Jess Nolan's around, too. The two of them are working up a rivalry and I got caught in the middle."

"And you got Kitty caught, too." That edge of anger returned.

"We agreed I should keep an eye on him, right?" she said. She brushed an arm against Ben, and he visibly calmed. "He hasn't shot anyone. Yet."

"Did either one of them try to hire you?" Ben said, in full interrogation mode now.

The Jeep's engine was still running. Cormac could drive away, right now.

"Layne did." The fact that he took Layne's money meant he'd essentially been hired. . . .

"You told him no, right?" Ben sighed, not bothering to wait for an answer. "Okay. Fine. I trust your judgment, and if you need to work with these guys to learn more—"

"I don't," Cormac said. "I'm done with them. I'm walking away and won't run into them again," he added.

"Seriously?"

"I'll figure out some other way to get at Crane's murder. Or get at Amy's book without help. I don't need these guys. You're right, they're trouble."

Ben might say he trusted Cormac, but that pause revealed a little too much uncertainty. Like they were still kids, right after Cormac's father died and everyone walked on eggshells around him, wondering when he was going to blow up.

"Good," Ben said finally.

His cousin might have been about to invite him in for a beer and further debriefing, but Cormac cut him off before he had the chance. "I'd better get going," he said, shifting the Jeep into reverse. "It's been a long couple of days."

"We'll talk later," Ben said.

"Yeah." He was used to being by himself, and he'd spent the whole day dealing with people. Enough was enough.

Kitty reached through the still-open window to squeeze his shoulder. "Be careful, okay? Get some ice on your face."

She turned to walk with Ben back to the house. A conventional ranch house at the edge of the suburbs that they paid for with their real jobs. They might have been werewolves, but they were more normal than he'd ever been.

You would never have chosen normal. Would you?

"Can't say I ever got the chance," he muttered, and swung the Jeep out of the driveway.

ON THE drive back to his apartment, he called Layne, who didn't answer. He left a message. "I tracked down your werewolf. He isn't. Nolan and his crew, they're just screwing around. You don't need to worry about them, I took care of it. If it'll make you feel better, have your guy put up protection charms against skinwalkers and keep a good watch. I don't need the second half of your bounty, and I don't need to sign up for your operation, whatever the hell you're doing. I'm out."

He'd spend tomorrow coming up with a plan B. Tonight—he deserved a cold beer and a long sleep in. At home, he started on the beer and would have forgotten about the ice on his face if Amelia hadn't reminded him. Enough time had passed—hours—ice probably wouldn't do any good. But he chanced a look in the bathroom mirror and the bruise had acquired a couple more colors in the intervening time. So he made up the ice pack and rested it over his eyes while he lay flat in bed.

He hardly had to think of it anymore. He closed his eyes, wanting to step out of his world. He wanted to talk to Amelia—and there they were. The meadow—dusk this time, a sunset like a lot of Colorado sunsets he'd stopped to look at, streaks of clouds glowing bright orange over shadowed mountains, bursts of fading sunlight breaking through.

He was sitting on his usual rock, looking over the creek. Amelia leaned in, doing the exact same thing Kitty had, wincing and reaching for his wounded face.

"I shouldn't have looked in the mirror. I wouldn't be picturing myself with a black eye then."

"But your body remembers," she said. She closed the last little distance, carefully touching his cheek. He flinched, but sat his ground. She wasn't real, but her touch was gentle, a warmth against the injured skin. "Does it hurt?"

"It's just sore."

"Something of a badge of honor, I suppose. What's next, then?" she asked.

"Exactly what I said. We find another way."

"You aren't the least bit curious about what the current Milo Kuzniak has to do with the old Milo Kuzniak and what kind of magic really is involved?"

"I'm curious, but it doesn't matter. We're moving on. I told Ben I wouldn't get wrapped up with those guys, so I won't."

She sat on her own chunk of granite, hands folded on her lap, regarding him. She wasn't happy, judging by her pinched expression. "I can't let a mystery like this go."

He knew that, had a shocking amount of experience with that now. The mystery of tracking down the vampire priest last year, the magic centered around Denver's Speedy Marts before that—Cormac would be living a nice, quiet life, except that Kitty kept bringing him problems to solve, and Amelia was too damned passionate about digging up the powers behind them.

"I can," he declared.

"That's not true. You're just as curious as I am. You hate a mystery, which means you can't stand letting it go unsolved. I just give you the means to solve it."

He didn't think he hated unsolved mysteries so much as he hated loose ends. "Well, what do you suggest?"

She licked her lips, leaned forward. "There's a spell. It's rather complex, but not difficult. The plateau where Crane was killed—we know there's residual magic there, we know some sort of power lingers. If we can gather the right materials—we'll have to go to Sand Creek, do you know about Sand Creek? I think we can draw out the information we need."

"What does this spell do?"

"It will re-create what happened—or a shadow of what happened. Perhaps then we'll learn how Crane died."

He didn't really want to know what Sand Creek had to do with this kind of spell, and he didn't want to go back to the plateau if it meant a chance of running into Layne again. The whole thing was more trouble than it was worth.

"It's a dead end," he said. "We keep after Layne and them, we're just going to keep running in circles. We'll find another way to decode Scanlon's book."

"I hardly care about the book anymore, I want to know how Milo Kuzniak killed Augustus Crane."

"So you can have that spell for yourself?"

She gave a curt nod. "Yes. And you do, too. How many times today did you wish for a gun that you didn't have? You won't need a gun to defend yourself if you have the right magic."

"I did just fine."

"What about the next time?"

"There isn't going to be a next time, that's the whole point."

"Cormac, don't you dare—"

He opened his eyes and sat up. The ice pack was dripping cold water everywhere, soaking his pillow. He went over to the kitchenette, tossed it in the sink, and stretched. Ignored Amelia poking at him, trying to change his mind.

He just wanted to get some sleep. He pulled off his T-shirt and jeans, stretched some of the ache out of his muscles, and collapsed back on the futon.

Chapter 15

LIFE WITH Cormac—as his would-be conscience, or perhaps rather a contrary imp riding on his shoulder—was certainly interesting. During that episode with the skinwalker she had thought they were about to find themselves in a real Old West shootout, a meeting between rogues like something out of the dime novels of her childhood. She had been thrilled by the whole thing. She feared Cormac was a bit annoyed by her.

She was very aware that she'd fallen victim—more than a hundred years ago—to the romantic allure of the American West. The daring tales, the exotic peoples, cowboys and Indians and all the rest. Adventure stories took place either in deepest Africa, or in the American West. She even saw Buffalo Bill's Wild West Show in London when she was a girl and had thought it very loud, with all the guns firing and horses stampeding and hundreds of participants yelling and whooping. She had absolutely adored watching Annie Oakley shoot. The woman could do absolutely anything, and so, Amelia decided, could she.

Of course, she would eventually travel to the American West to see it all for herself. What she hadn't quite realized—but would have, had she thought about it without the emotional dreams of adventure—was that the Wild West of Buffalo Bill's show had long ago vanished, and had never really existed at all in that stylized form. The Indians now lived impoverished, their native dignity all but vanished after the wars that forced them to the reservations. Real cowboys were coarse rather than heroic. Those so-called frontier towns all had train stations, churches, universities, well-stocked shops, fine ladies in corsets and men in smart hats and ties, and rows of fancy houses, just like any other town in any other civilized part of the world.

Her own adventure in the American West had ended very badly, as it happened. She should have known.

Before then, when she finally met a real Indian face-to-face in the genuine Old West, the encounter was not what she expected. He was an old man sitting in a chair outside of a photography studio in Colorado Springs. He wore a much-washed button-up shirt, dungarees, and had wrapped a battered Indian-woven blanket around his shoulders against a chill in the air. His only gestures toward a legendary appearance were his long hair, ebony streaked with gray, kept in two braids over his shoulders, and a beaded headband with a feather tied to it. A sign in the window of the studio announced that one could pay ten cents to have one's picture taken with a real Indian. Amelia declined, but spoke with the man for a few moments.

"Sir, do you speak English?" she said clearly to him. "Might I have a word with you?"

"You might need more than one," he answered, without a smile. His accent was American, which surprised her, and she realized that in truth she hadn't known what to expect at all.

"I'm from England," she said. "I'm interested in learning all I can about this region. What tribe are you from, sir? Where do you come from?"

He might have smiled, by the way the furrows in his face shifted. He nodded, indicating the street behind her. "I'm from here."

"You were born here in the city?" she responded, confused.

"Wasn't a city then."

"Where is your tribe now? I would like to meet a medicine man—if you could perhaps introduce me to someone who might be able to teach me—"

"Ma'am," he said curtly. "He's dead. Everybody's dead. There's no one left. I can't help you." He looked away and tugged the blanket more tightly around his shoulders.

She straightened, taken aback. What she had taken for sadness in the drawn look in his face, the shadows in his eyes, she now saw was anger. A futile anger that had been buried for a long time.

Before she could make another attempt to question him, a smartly dressed couple came to the shop, eager to have their picture taken with a real Indian. His services required, he went into the shop at the photographer's command, and Amelia was left staring at the rough chair where he'd been sitting, wondering why she felt queasy.

She did more research, asking and reading, learning what Indian tribes had been located in the area before the city was founded. There were many, Cheyenne and Arapaho, with other tribes passing through—Ute, Kiowa, Comanche. She had no idea there were so many different tribes. She'd only known about the Sioux of the plains, featured so vividly in the Wild West Show, and the Pueblo of the southwest, with their fascinating clay-built dwellings. So much to learn, and she only had the barest scraps of knowledge to go on: stories of strange magic, medicine men who transformed into animals and entered other worlds, hints of mystical healing. They would tell her that if she had not been raised in their tribes, grown up with their knowledge, then she couldn't possibly gain access to it now. But she would convince them, she had to convince them.

Then she learned about Sand Creek. The old Indian at the photography shop said everyone was dead. It seemed he did not exaggerate. She knew, then, that no Indian medicine man, even if she could find one still living, would ever help her, a white woman, learn their secrets. She could not blame them for refusing her.

People told ghost stories about Sand Creek, and even if she never learned a scrap of Indian magic, she wanted to follow the thread of inquiry to its end.

She traveled to Lamar by train, then hired a horse to make the rest of the journey. She brought little with her—a dowsing rod, some candles and sage for dispelling, and a charm meant to attract ghosts. Mainly she wanted to observe. She'd never stopped hunting for fairies.

She'd been told this spot of land was haunted, that you could not step onto it without feeling the misery, the abject tragedy of what had happened. She'd been told one could see the ghosts rising from the ground where the massacre had taken place. Some still called it the Battle of Sand Creek, but more and more the word "massacre" superseded the previous title. After all, one could hardly call it a battle when one of the two sides had laid down their weapons.

A full moon rose over the prairie. It was still several hours until midnight, but she'd been walking an hour already, guiding her horse along a likely path. She hadn't asked for specific directions because she didn't want to know; if this place really was so powerful, she ought to be able to feel the spirits.

When the hired horse planted its feet, shying away from an invisible spot ahead, she stopped and set up her little camp, feeding and hobbling the horse, spreading her bedroll, and making a fire to boil water for tea.

She stayed calm and breathed deeply, letting her senses, her presence, her mind, settle into the place. A cold wind blew. Sitting on the blanket, she wrapped her coat and another blanket around her and moved close to the fire. She wasn't going to get any sleep, which was fine, that wasn't her purpose here. Nearby, her horse shuffled in its hobbles and nibbled at the dried winter grasses, a calming noise against the wind. Patches of snow lay here and there, left over from the last storm and glowing silver in the moonlight. This far east, at night, the mountains of the Front Range weren't visible. Nothing but prairie and farmland all around her.

The horse, she noticed, wouldn't move any further north than the spot where she'd made her fire. It wandered back and forth, never straying far, but only on one side of her camp. She directed her attention north, then. Peeling out of her warm blankets, she went to her saddlebag, found the right charm, and lit the candle from a brand she took from the fire. Moving a little ways off, turning her back to the fire and letting her eyesight adjust to the night, she set the candle on a clear space of ground, clasped the charm between her hands, and murmured the words to waken it.

She reached up and swiped her hand across the air as if she were pulling back a curtain—a metaphorical action, but one with consequences.

Still, nothing but a faint wind rustled the grasses and moonlight.

She spoke softly, carefully. "I would like to talk to you. I know a great wrong was done to you and you have no reason to listen to me, to trust me. But my intentions are good, I think you'll find. I simply want to learn—"

A gun fired, a sound like a single concentrated crack of thunder, painful to her ears. Then another fired, and another, then many, all at once. Nothing at all like the Wild West Show, this was the sound of war, of being in the middle of a battle and having the world explode around you. She wondered how soldiers stood it, their ears tearing apart while they raised their own weapons and hoped to function as they'd trained. All she could do was squeeze hands over her head and curl up on the ground, hoping to protect herself from this onslaught.

But there was no battle. No shouting, no men bearing rifles, no smell of burning gunpowder. Just the noise, the ghost of long-ago events. She did, however, catch a faint scent of blood.

She grabbed her bundle of sage, lit it from the embers of her fire, and swept its pungent, earthy smoke all around her. *"Aufere, aufere, aufere!"*

The horse shied, hopped a step, then settled back to grazing. It hadn't heard any gunfire or it would have bolted, hobbles or no.

There was no gunfire, no phantom sounds or smells. The prairie was silent again. It wasn't real. But something had happened—not ghosts, maybe. But something.

She stayed at her camp until dawn, but she didn't sleep. Sitting wrapped in her blanket, she fed twigs into the fire to keep it burning low, and looked out at the prairie, her ears still ringing from phantom gunfire. Dawn came slowly.

After packing her things and brushing and saddling her horse, she took a few moments to walk around the site, stepping carefully on hard-packed soil, last year's dried grasses catching on the hem of her skirt. The massacre had happened more than forty years ago. A generation. But that old man—he could have been a boy here. No physical sign of the Indian camp, of what had happened here, remained. The prairie, the wind and the dust blowing over it, had obscured it all. Only memories remained. Memories and shadows.

Her toe hit against something with a metallic clink.

She knelt, searched, found what her step had dislodged: a brass bullet casing, weathered and corroded. It had obviously been lying here, half buried, for years. When she lifted it, it felt much heavier than it should have. As if the bullet was still housed in it, as if the weight of what the bullet had done still clung to it.

Of course, there was no way to tell that this came from a gun that had been used in the massacre. Forty years had passed, forty years of people crossing this patch of ground for any number of reasons. No reason to think this particular casing was cursed.

She put it in her pouch and would think on this further.

SO MUCH for the romance of the American West. Anderson Layne, Jess Nolan, all of them were a pale shadow of those old days. No, that wasn't right. These days, these people were probably not so very different at all. Just as venal, just as criminal. These days simply hadn't had time to gain a veneer of romance. No one had yet told any thrilling tales of men like Anderson Layne.

She had thought to use the casing she'd found at Sand Creek for some kind of charm or talisman. Even if it hadn't been used in the massacre, the fact of its age, of its lying in such a place of power, would give it some small usefulness. But she never got the chance.

She didn't know what happened to her belongings after her arrest. Confiscated and given away, she imagined. Thrown in a trash heap. This was why returning to her childhood home to retrieve what few things she'd left behind there had become so important, last year when Cormac went to London with Kitty. It had been a small treasure hunt, but such a large prize, because it was all she had.

HIS RINGING phone woke Cormac up. He took a long time to crawl to wakefulness, as if the ringtone was some thread from a dream, not at all real, and his conscious mind dismissed it. But it didn't stop. He grabbed his phone from the crate he used as a bedside table. Three A.M. The number wasn't Kitty or Ben calling, which meant it wasn't an emergency as far as he was concerned.

He answered anyway, and Layne talked at him. "Bennett, oh God, Bennett, you have to get over here."

Cormac flopped back on the bed, stared at the ceiling, and bit back a curse. "Did you get my message?"

"No . . . no, there's no time for that, you don't understand—"

"I can't help you," Cormac said. "I'm not working for you. Leave me out of your shit."

"But—but this is crazy! I don't know anyone else who can help!"

"What about your guy, Kuzniak? Let him figure it out." He almost hung up at that, but Layne let out a wail.

"That's just it! He's dead! He's been killed!"

Chapter 16

BY DAWN, he was driving back down the freeway.

Perhaps Nolan and company aren't as harmless as we thought.

He didn't have a clue. But a guy named Milo Kuzniak dying under mysterious circumstances—he had to check it out. Layne hadn't been able to tell him much, just that Milo didn't have a mark on him, which ruled out Eddie the skinwalker and Nolan's rifle, and nobody knew what had happened. Cormac had told him to call the police, let them investigate. But that would have invited scrutiny of everything else Layne had going on at his compound. So, no, he would not call the police. He wanted Cormac.

Cormac kept thinking he should have refused to help. But he also thought he could stick around just long enough to get an idea about what happened. Maybe he'd find the key to the whole damned puzzle.

Amelia had him pack a few things, different odds

and ends than what he usually carried around in his pockets: red pillar candles and a round, frameless mirror. There was something familiar about the items, but it was from one of her memories, not his, and she was keeping thoughts about it to herself. Something he ought to learn to do, since she always seemed to be able to tell exactly what he was thinking.

Because you're very emotional. You do a good job of hiding it from everyone, but behind all that you're rather a mess.

Last thing he needed was the back of his own head psychoanalyzing him. He knew he was a mess. He dealt with it. He turned up the radio in the Jeep so he wouldn't have to hear himself think.

The sun was up and burning off the winter chill when he arrived at Layne's compound. He turned into the drive, ready to roll all the way to the front of the house, but a body lay in the middle of the dirt tracks. Milo Kuzniak the younger, splayed face up, arms and legs spread out, no obvious signs of violence on the body.

He considered slamming the Jeep into reverse and getting the hell out. This—approaching a potential crime scene, disturbing a crime scene with no intention of telling the cops about it—was *exactly* the kind of thing Ben and Kitty were worried about him getting into. This could get him thrown back in jail.

You have gloves, yes?

Sometimes, he wondered if Amelia wasn't worse than he was. He found his leather gloves shoved on the dashboard.

Layne had been watching for him. He came walking up from the house as soon as Cormac left the Jeep, and had a rifle tucked under his arm. Cormac glanced at the house, wondering if Mollie was around. He hoped not, what with people dying and all. He ignored Layne and went to the body.

Cormac wasn't a forensics guy. He'd read a couple of books because Amelia wanted to learn, and he figured, why not. Mostly, it told him where the TV shows got everything wrong. But he knew a little. The body's stiffness meant Milo had been lying here for a while, but he hadn't started to stink. His eyes were open, his lips slack. No blood, no wounds, no nothing. The guy looked smaller, somehow.

He questioned Amelia: did magic do this?

We'll find out.

"Thanks for coming," Layne said, which was decent of him. He seemed a lot calmer now than he had on the phone. The panic had subsided. That made Cormac suspicious.

"I ought to just keep driving, Layne. I'm doing you a favor."

"I figure I paid you enough for the werewolf job, I earned a little extra work from you."

That was exactly what Cormac thought he'd say.

He gave Layne a look and stepped up to the body. He studied the surrounding area for anything out of place, signs of violence, a fight, or magic. As it was, Milo might have had a heart attack and fallen over. This needed a coroner, not a magician.

Kneeling by the body, he looked closer. Maybe not a heart attack—he didn't look like he'd died in pain. He wasn't tense, curled up—his muscles hadn't been clenched. Really, the guy looked like he'd been surprised. He hadn't even had time to turn around. Something had happened that he hadn't expected, and it had been instantaneous.

Milo's arms were outstretched, his hands turned up, and soot streaked his palms, as if he'd held an exploding firecracker. Or put his hands up to fend off an attack.

Cormac looked up at Layne, who stood a ways off, refusing to approach the body. "You see what happened?"

"No." He crossed his arms. "I was expecting Nolan's crew to come back and pull some other stunt, so we were all awake, keeping watch. Milo was out front here, all by himself. There was a bang, like somebody setting off a bomb, and I came running. Nothing was there, not even a puff of smoke, and Milo was dead, just like that. They did something to him, didn't they? Nolan and his werewolf?"

The story didn't sound right. Kuzniak wasn't one

of Layne's heavies. He didn't even carry a gun. He wouldn't have been keeping watch at the end of the driveway all by himself.

Nolan didn't do this, Cormac was sure. Dumb as he was, the guy wasn't dumb enough to come after Layne on his own ground. He would have sent Eddie, and Eddie would have just torn the guy up. Even if Kuzniak had been out here by himself.

Layne wasn't telling everything that happened. Of course he wasn't.

"Did you listen to the message I left you?" Cormac asked.

"Not yet—"

"Nolan doesn't have a werewolf working for him. Nolan didn't do this. You're being paranoid."

"Easy for you to say. Can you tell me what happened or not?"

There's a way to learn more. He wasn't sure he wanted to know, but he didn't have any other ideas.

"I still think you should call the cops." He couldn't believe he was saying this, but missing people and dead bodies drew attention sooner or later and Cormac didn't want to be stuck in the middle of this.

"I am not calling the cops."

"Then I take it you have a hole to drop him into?"

"Of course." He sounded offended.

Right. What now? he asked Amelia. *We'll need privacy.*

"You go back to the house. I'll let you know what I find."

"What are you going to do?"

He glared. "You want me to do this or not? Go back to the house."

Still nervous, still gripping the rifle like he'd be happy to use it if he just had a target, Layne shuffled back on the gravel drive. Cormac watched him go, all the way to the house's porch.

"He's going to keep watching, you know," Cormac murmured.

Yes, but at least his paranoia will be far away from here. And really, we don't want him to see this.

Dead body. Mirror. Candles. "Wait a minute—"

Just let me do this. Please?

"Goddammit," he muttered.

Get the chalk and candles. First, we'll need a circle.

This was what Amelia'd been doing with Lydia Harcourt when she'd been arrested: questioning the body about its own murder. Convenient.

He followed her instructions. They'd worked together enough that he knew about protective circles—they didn't just keep the magician safe while she was working her spell, but they also kept the sometimes dangerous energies from escaping and causing harm. Amelia was careful with her protections, and Cormac took his time marking out the circle, both with ground-up chalk that he kept in a jar in the Jeep, and also with the candles. The thing started looking downright sinister, and he wondered what Layne back at the house was making of it.

Pay attention, if you please.

One of these days, he was going to lose his temper at her and just walk away from this shit. And she'd stick right there with him. He could ignore her—but she'd invade his dreams and stand there, scowling at him. He couldn't get away.

He was going to need a drink after this.

Perhaps it's time you simply let me take charge of this.

Fine with him. Without her knowledge and experience, he could only do so much. So he stepped back.

He'd gotten used to the feeling, like he was dreaming while also being awake. He watched through his own eyes as his hands moved, his body turned, and his senses dimmed. It should have been terrifying, but it was like hunting predators, bears and wolves and the like, with the ability to turn on you and maul you to death: you couldn't panic. Simple as that. Stay calm, keep breathing, get through it.

She always stepped aside when she finished whatever magic she was working. He kept watch, ready to take action if he needed to.

"You should trust me by now," she spoke, using his voice. The sound was his, but the words and syntax were not.

He didn't trust anyone. She knew that.

She pulled out the mirror she'd had him pack, laid it by the body's head. Lit candles, burned incense, whispered words of invocation.

He felt it. Even if he hadn't been watching for it, he would have felt the power rise from the ground itself, a tingling across his skin, a prickling as individual hairs rose on his scalp. This wasn't scrying. Not exactly. This wasn't just trying to read an imprint of whatever magic had happened here, this wasn't just tracking the lines of power—she wouldn't have needed so much ritual for that. This was something else, something more.

Knowing abstractly what was going to happen and seeing it happen were two different things. When the power rose, feeling like the whole universe was going off kilter, he almost let the panic take hold. He wanted to run. Kick her out of his mind and get the hell away.

The dead body moved. The faintest flush passed through it.

"It's all right," she murmured. To the body, not to him. He held his breath, waiting.

The mirror fogged, as if hot breath blew across it. Breath from the body. Then the eyes blinked, and lips pressed together. Brief flickers of movement. Amelia murmured, "Shh, it's all right, Milo. Just a question or two, then you can rest."

He blinked again; his eyes were shining, moisture gathering in them. Tears, maybe.

"Milo Kuzniak," she said. "I know you can hear me. I need to know what happened to you."

The lips worked, struggling to form words. Amelia leaned close.

Of all Cormac had seen in his life, this was the first thing he'd ever thought to call horrifying. She'd called the man's soul back to interrogate him—and he was in pain.

The mirror fogged with breath again, and he spoke in a wheezing whisper.

"Back. It came back. It came back." Lydia Harcourt's throat had been cut deep; she hadn't been able to speak when Amelia summoned her a hundred years ago. Kuzniak could, and it sounded wrong.

"What came back, Milo?" Amelia said, gently as she could, but clearly impatient. "Was there a creature? One of your enemies? Was it Jess Nolan and his skinwalker?"

He—the body—grimaced, his whole face contorting with grief or pain or terror. He could talk, enough of him had been drawn back to his body that he was aware—but he couldn't move. He had no power.

"Pocket. Book. Pocket." A low keening started in his throat, a scream that couldn't break loose. He bared his teeth, as if an electric shock traveled through his body. Still, only his expression stirred. His body was dead. But what was speaking?

"Milo—stay with me. I want to know who did this to you. Help me learn who did this, and how."

"No one." The words hissed, then the lips clamped shut.

The light sputtered; the candles around the circle had burned down to stubs in just a few minutes. Soon, they'd burn out.

Amelia said, "Do you have any messages? Anyone you'd like to say good-bye to? I'll pass along any words for you, if I'm able."

"No one. No one."

The fog across the mirror's surface vanished, and Milo Kuzniak's face went slack. Dead, absolutely dead. His eyes were closed.

Cormac's stomach was turning, and he wasn't sure any of this had been worth it. Three sentences and a lot of pain.

Damn, Amelia murmured.

She slipped away, and Cormac's body was his own again. His skin tingled, his muscles clenched. He stretched his gloved fingers, rolled his shoulders back, and took a deep breath. He was back behind the wheel, taking over from a lousy driver.

It's not so bad, is it?

None of what dead Milo had said made any sense.

Something had come back, something about a pocket book—or just a pocket. Cormac tipped the body on its side to pat down the overcoat, jeans, feeling in the front and back pockets. And there it was. His little moleskin notebook, worn around the edges, elastic around the cover stretched out, pages dog-eared.

Another damned book of shadows, he'd bet. He slipped the book into his own pocket to look at later. Another mystery, another secret, and maybe they had a chance of finding the answer *this* time. As long as he hadn't written in code. Cormac resisted an urge to stand up and kick the body, just in case he'd feel like doing it later.

Instead, he cleaned up after the spell, gathering the mirror and candle remnants, brushing the chalk circle into oblivion with his boot.

"What the hell was that?" Cormac muttered. A rhetorical question mostly, but directed at Amelia. "Fucking necromancy?"

She wasn't apologetic. *I haven't worked that spell since I was arrested. I wasn't sure I'd be able to.*

"Then was that me panicking, or you?"

She didn't answer.

"So, what is it? A ghost, haunting their body? Their souls? Does the spell trap them?"

I'm . . . not entirely sure.

"You don't know what happens to them after? You're chaining some kind of spirit to their body and pulling their strings, and you don't know? You might be trapping them, torturing them—you stop to think that Lydia Harcourt's ghost may really be haunting that house in Manitou, after what you did to her?"

Silence. He couldn't even feel her lurking.

Layne was walking back up the drive. Show was over.

"Well?" the man asked.

Something wasn't right here. "I still need to do some checking around. I'll let you know what I find."

"But what killed him? Is it going to happen again?"

"I don't know," Cormac said.

"Then what good are you?"

"I never said I was any good, you just assumed."

If it helps, I don't think it will happen again. I think this was something that targeted magicians, someone who was working spells.

So where does that put us? Cormac asked. "I don't think it'll happen again. Looks like what got him might have been magic gone wrong. Avoid magic, you'll be fine," he said to Layne. "Keep an eye out, though."

"Okay. Good. I believe you. Oh, and I'll take that book you found in Milo's pocket."

So he'd definitely been watching. Cormac thought about responding with, "What book?" Just to see the look on Layne's face, and just to see what the guy would do about it. But he was supposed to be walking away from all this. Might as well just let him have it.

Amelia did panic at this. *No, he can't have it, he wouldn't even know what to do with it. We have to know what Milo was working on—*

Layne put out his hand. "Give it. Now."

"You think you'll know what to do with it? You know anything about spell books?"

Layne's eyes widened, a flash of surprise, of hunger. He hadn't known what it was, but now he did, and he wanted it.

I *want it!*

A headache started pounding behind Cormac's ears, throbbing dully. He hadn't had one like this since he was back in prison, when Amelia was first trying to break into his mind. This was her, fighting back.

Layne was an idiot. He was going to get himself in trouble. Cormac decided he didn't much care. He pulled the book out of his pocket and handed it over.

"This means you don't call me again. If you do, I'm not going to come running." He walked away, back to the Jeep. Amelia grumbled at him the whole time.

"Whatever you say."

Two of the henchmen came up from the house. Cormac watched from the Jeep, morbidly curious about how they were getting rid of the body. He expected Layne had a ditch somewhere, an old mine shaft or even just a cave, and that Milo wasn't the first body to get tossed there. If it was on private property, no one would ever find it to be able to report it, and if Milo didn't have anyone around to declare him missing—well then, he was as good as gone.

Milo couldn't have expected to end up that way. But you spend enough time with a guy like Layne, well . . .

Which was why Cormac was driving away.

Milo was telling us what he was doing, what killed him, it's all in the book, I must have that book!

Cormac didn't want to argue. He was thinking more about how this—disappearing down some backwoods hole, dead and lost—could never happen to him. Ben wouldn't let it. Hell, neither would Kitty. Strangely comforting, having people watching his back. He drove, glancing in the rearview mirror to see the guys hauling the body, arms slung over their shoulders, down to the woods at the back of the property.

Ten or so miles later, when the gravel county road met asphalt, he pulled over and parked on the shoulder. The headache was pounding now, Amelia refusing to be ignored.

"What?" he said out loud.

We cannot walk away from this.

"Yes, we can. I just did."

He leaned back against the seat, tipped his head back, closed his eyes. He could fall asleep, right here.

The bruise around his eye throbbed in time with his pulse. The headache didn't dim.

If you won't go back for Kuzniak's book, the only way to learn more about Kuzniak and Crane is to go to the plateau and work the Sand Creek spell to re-create what happened, perhaps even summon Crane's spirit—

"No. No more summoning. No more talking to dead people."

One might think you were squeamish.

"I just know better than to go sticking my head where it doesn't belong."

You're a coward.

Almost sounded like his father saying that. Time was, he'd start a fight over those words.

Cormac. Come and talk to me. Don't shut me out like this, I can't stand it.

He caught a whiff of fear at that. She argued because she was stubborn, but while she did she worried—how precarious was her place here, really?

Sometimes he thought about what it would take to get rid of her. If he thought hard enough, if he found the right spell or incantation—hell, if he ignored her long enough—could he eject her spirit? Just kick her out, to dissipate on the wind or astral plane or whatever happened to spirits that didn't have bodies. Or would she find some other way to bother him. Haunting his

Jeep, maybe, shorting out spark plugs whenever she disagreed with him. So yes, the situation with Amelia *could* be much more annoying that it was now.

Without her, the apartment would be very quiet.

Cormac. Please come and talk to me, face-to-face.

He let out a breath and fell into their mental space, his memory turned real. He was standing in the middle of a damp meadow, looking around for her. The place was cold this time. A sharp, wet wind was blowing, the kind that came through the mountains in autumn, smelling of impending snow. Cormac shivered, wondering why he couldn't just make a wish and bring back summer. This was all in his head. But the bad weather reflected his mood. Both their moods.

The trees across the valley swayed in the wind, the trunks creaking.

Amelia appeared, just far enough away that she had to raise her voice to be heard. She stood primly, as if she were arguing her case in court. "Without Kuzniak's book, without learning what happened to him, our options are limited."

"I already told you the option I pick—quit the whole thing."

"I think we should go back to the plateau." She seemed unaffected by the chill, maybe because her old-fashioned gown with its thick wool and high collar kept her warm. Maybe because she didn't have a body anymore, she couldn't feel the cold. "I want to try *my* spell."

"No. It's not right. The dead should stay dead. Let them lie, don't scare them up and try to talk to them, don't bring back the past." He looked across the way, studying the clouds rolling in from the west, gauging what the weather was going to do next. As if it were real weather.

Amelia moved around him, putting herself in his line of sight, trying to catch his gaze. He kept looking out to the wild, which he understood better.

"If I didn't know you, I'd say you were having moral qualms. What are you afraid of?"

"I'm not afraid. It's just wrong."

"Are you afraid your own dead will rise up to speak to you? To berate you? How many people have you killed, Cormac? Including the monsters. You've never told me that. You never let that knowledge slip out."

He'd never told anyone. Not even Ben knew all the hunts he'd been on, all the contracts he'd taken, the exact number of people he'd killed. He'd never asked. Amelia was the first person who had.

He knew the number without having to stop and count. "Eighteen."

She didn't seem at all horrified. Just nodded thoughtfully. "The first was the werewolf who killed your father, when you were sixteen? And the latest was the skinwalker, the one that put you in prison?"

"There was the demon back in prison. And the werewolf in Chinatown, the one I stabbed. He's eighteen."

"You count the demon as one of your kills?"

"It was sentient. Devious. It was a hunter. Maybe it wasn't a human being, but it wasn't an easy kill, so why not count it?"

She raised an eyebrow. "One might make an argument that it was *my* kill, not yours."

"All right—seventeen and a half kills, that make you happy?"

"Fair enough. The rest of them—were they all vampires and werewolves and other monsters? Have you ever killed a mortal, normal human?"

"Two. Two of those were human."

"Any regrets?"

"No. They all deserved to die. I'm pretty sure they did." Even the one who'd just gotten in the way had chosen to be there, had known what would happen if he stayed. That was what Cormac figured.

"Then why do the dead haunt you? Why are you afraid of speaking to them?"

Her questions, her pushing him, made his neck stiff. Caused an itching deep in his spine, and he wanted to swat at the bugs crawling there. He walked. Realized he was pacing, like a predator in a cage, and didn't much care. Kept going, down the sloping hill along the creek. But this wasn't reality, wasn't a physical space, and Amelia appeared at his side, keeping pace with him. Studying him. He didn't turn to look at her.

"Cormac?"

It wasn't the dead that scared him. He wasn't afraid of hearing from any of the people he'd killed. When he couldn't sleep at night, it wasn't any of their voices he heard, keeping him awake.

"Cormac," she said. "Your walls are going up again."

He hadn't realized he was doing it. In prison, when she'd first tried to contact him, her spirit edging its way into his mind, he'd resisted. He'd built walls, imagined them going up stone by stone to keep her out. She'd almost driven him crazy, trying to break through. He'd finally let her in so they could stop the demon that was killing prisoners.

The wind, the freezing snow—his mind was going cold.

He said, then, "My father." He stopped walking, still couldn't look at her. But he could at least stop trying to escape.

"If you start speaking to the dead . . . you're afraid you would have to start speaking to him."

He didn't even have to channel the man's spirit. Cormac heard his voice berating him for getting caught, for going soft, for not being good enough, for not being *good.* Right after he was attacked and infected with lycanthropy, Ben had wanted Cormac to shoot him. Being a monster was supposed to be worse than being dead. But Kitty changed that. Cormac refused to kill Ben, and the world was better for it.

Douglas Bennett would have killed Ben without hesitating.

Cormac was weak, and he imagined his father's ghost whispered to him. He was *wrong.* He'd been given a legacy, an inheritance to protect the world from monsters. And now, he was shirking his duties, working with the monsters instead of killing them. He was just about a monster himself. A guy with two auras and a pocketful of magic spells.

He didn't have to speak any of this out loud to Amelia. She sensed it pouring out of him. The walls were down.

"That voice isn't real, you know," she said. "It's your imagination. I'm sure he wouldn't be so . . . so judgmental."

"You didn't know him."

"No, I only have your memories to go on. The memories of a sixteen-year-old boy—not entirely reliable, if I may say so. If it would lay his spirit to rest in your mind, we could try to channel him. Just to see."

He shook his head. No. Just no. He didn't need to do that. His father was wrong, he was moving forward, that was all.

Amelia stepped closer, her manner oddly hesitant. "Perhaps . . . there are other ways of laying spirits to rest. I—I would like to see the place where he died. Have you ever been back there, since it happened?"

"No."

She put a hand on his shoulder. The gesture felt strangely tangible, her touch warm and gentle. "Let's go, why don't we?"

And why not? He needed to take a walk. He needed to get out of here.

Chapter 17

HE COULDN'T find the spot.

With a burning desire to stay out of the whole of southern Colorado for the next few days, he drove up to Grand County, to the ranch where Douglas Bennett had died.

They'd gotten a call from the owner that something crazy was going on—cattle slaughtered in that distinctive way by something more than wild—and crazy was what the Bennett clan did. It had been a full moon that night.

He didn't know anymore who owned the land at this spot bordering the Arapaho National Forest, but he found the back road he and his father had taken there, mostly by trusting instinct and memory. Along the way, with a mile or so left to go, the charred remains of a forest started. Instead of trees, blackened spikes jutted from ash-covered ground. The air smelled like a dusty fireplace. The place was wet, muddy from new snow, a soppy mess. The fire had been recent—not even the scrub oak had had a chance to grow back. The forest's remains were skeletal.

This must have been the edge of the Church's Park Fire that took out around five hundred acres of forest last fall. He remembered hearing about it, wondering vaguely if the fire's range approached the area where he and his father had spent so much time. He assumed not and never bothered looking at a map. So much for that. He hadn't really thought about what that meant, if his father's old territory had burned down.

The road dwindled to a couple of pale tracks on the dark, ash-laden earth, so he parked the Jeep and started walking. He was pretty sure he was in the right spot. The shape of the hills looked familiar, but the trees and clearings he might have recognized were gone. Nothing but charcoal underfoot. He kicked and raised a cloud of ash.

It's rather desolate.

"It wasn't like this back then."

He walked until he thought he'd gone far enough, but didn't trust his sense of distance. The last time he'd been here, running back after calling the cops, showing them where the whole thing had happened, he felt like he'd been running forever, sucking down breaths, on the edge of crying. Realizing he had blood spatters on him, spray from the werewolf he'd shot. If he walked for as long as he thought he'd been running that night, he'd end up on the other side of the county.

You can't expect to remember exactly where it was, in the middle of wilderness. It's been over twenty years, Cormac.

"That long, huh?"

He remembered what the blood smelled like. He could hear his father explaining: hunting the monsters—this'll be your job when I'm gone. How many monsters have you killed, son? More important, how many *haven't* you killed?

Kitty, Ben, their whole pack, Denver's vampire Family, the vampire Families in D.C., San Francisco, and London, not to mention the werewolves in those cities. He'd let them all live. Hundreds of monsters he hadn't killed. Just because they were Kitty's friends, and Kitty had convinced him that even monsters deserved a chance.

None of those people had hurt anyone, Amelia murmured to him. *They're good people, you know they are.*

Looking around, he couldn't see it. The place his father died hadn't looked like this. Maybe he should have come back at night, under a full moon. Maybe then it would look familiar.

"The valley we camped in sometimes, the one I see in my mind, where we talk together—it's near here. In the back country, maybe ten miles off." Even if it hadn't burned down in some wildfire, the forest might have been replaced by dead beetle-killed pines, developers might have moved in to turn the place into condos. Anything could have happened. The old scenes slipped away.

Amelia said, *That place—perhaps you shouldn't go back there. You should keep that memory the way it is, the way it lives in your mind.*

She was right. He turned to leave.

Wait a moment. Do we still have any sage? And a stone—that piece of slate? I think I remember there being a shard of slate, left pocket.

She was right, of course, and he drew out the two items, feeling awkward. "I said I didn't want to do any channeling—"

This isn't. It's not even a spell, really. It's . . . a ritual. A very minor ritual. Come now, light the incense.

He lit the sprig of sage, blew to set it smoldering. "What's this supposed to do?"

It lays spirits to rest. It brings closure. You need to let your father go, Cormac.

He had. A long time ago. Or, he thought he had. But at her words, something inside him loosened, as if a fist had been holding tightly to his breath and now it finally opened.

She murmured words—phrases about releasing tension and moving on, wishing the best for someone long gone. Declaring that regrets were useless, and thus abandoning them. It wasn't an incantation or a spell, but more like a prayer. He wondered if it would still work, given he didn't much believe in any of the available gods. He hadn't been in a church outside a professional capacity since he was a boy.

You don't have to believe in anything. It's meant to make you feel better. That's all this is.

New Age crap. He didn't have much time for it.

Now, dig a hole. A small one will do, just knock the dirt away with your heel.

He did as she asked, stomped a couple of times to make a crescent-shaped hole.

Now, drop the stone in, and think about your father at peace. You have to hold the thought.

The burning sage was filling his nose, making his sinuses itch. But he dropped the stone in, and spread the dirt back over it with his hand.

"Good-bye, Dad," he murmured.

The sage stopped burning, the embers fading and smoke vanishing. A bird was calling somewhere, probably a jay. Somehow, he felt lighter.

Let's go, then.

AMELIA WAS very quiet on the drive back. She didn't bring up ghosts, scrying, or speaking with the dead. About getting their hands on Kuzniak's book, or what the hell they were going to do about solving Crane's murder for Judi and Frida. Made for a peaceful couple of hours, really. And a good night's sleep afterward. He almost poked at her, to make sure she was still there. But he didn't have to; she was always there, lurking.

Morning gave him a clean perspective, on everything. Layne was an ass, and he was fucking around with things he didn't understand. Treating magic like a fancy new automatic rifle he could buy under the table and show off to make himself a big man. A rifle just shot people up, but magic could raise the dead, summon demons. Destroy the world, if Kitty's paranoia was right. Milo Kuzniak was only one casualty. Maybe not even the first. Mollie was staying in that house, too, and he didn't want her caught up in this if Layne lit a fuse he couldn't put out.

Cormac didn't care about the mysteries quite so much, but he was going to make sure Layne's ambitions didn't go any further than they were right now. Put the bastard back in his place.

I thought a good night's sleep might help, Amelia said innocently. *If I may ask—what exactly are you planning to do?*

"We're going to get Milo Kuzniak's book."

Chapter 18

CORMAC WASN'T going to risk the trouble he might bring down on himself by carrying a gun, but he had other options. He made sure to put an extra gas can in the Jeep and threw a bottle of lighter fluid and extra flares in his road kit. Rope, bungee cord, duct tape, paper towels, empty soda bottles, a filled canteen. A regular catalog of useful items.

I have spells, Amelia said. *Charms. They won't turn you invisible, but they'll turn attention from you. They'll quiet your steps. Protect you from magical shields—*

He sensed that she was disturbed by some of what he was collecting. They weren't magical, which meant she didn't know what to do with them.

"No. We're doing this the old-fashioned way. *My* old-fashioned, not yours."

Oh, dear.

He got some sense of satisfaction when a tidbit

came up on the regional news—he hadn't expected it to rate major coverage, so he was happy to see anything about it at all. The headline read: "Two Area Men Arrested, Arsenal Confiscated." Nolan and Eddie were being held in the county jail pending a hearing in federal court, likely on charges of misuse of federal land and illegal weapons possession. Nothing serious, but it would definitely keep the pair out of everyone's hair for a while. Eddie couldn't even do anything about it while he was in jail—without his animal skins, he was powerless.

This also meant they hadn't had anything to do with Kuzniak's death, confirming Cormac's suspicion.

He headed back to Layne's compound. Felt good, doing this on his own terms. Doing something decisive.

Well after dark, still a mile away from the compound, he left the road, gathered up a choice selection of equipment, and took a path through the woods, stepping carefully, using his small flashlight to watch the undergrowth for obstacles. When he reached Layne's compound, he took care to carefully push down the barbed wire with gloved hands, so he could cross the fence. Hidden in the trees, he watched the house for whatever guard or patrol Layne had set up, if any.

For the most part, the place was still. No movement

at the barn or the surrounding acreage. A couple of lights on in the house, but again no movement. A few of Layne's crew must have been staying here, based on the cars in the drive. He decided Mollie probably wasn't here—he hadn't seen her last time. He had to assume there was some kind of alarm system—regular, not magical. He wondered if it just covered the house, or the driveway as well. Layne didn't have an active guard, nobody walking patrol or anything. Even after Kuzniak getting killed, the remote location must have made Layne feel safe. Any of Kuzniak's protection spells would have died with him. Physical charms he might have placed might still be working.

He needed a distraction to get the guys out of the house. A big one. *Without* using any magic. He was leery enough of starting something that would rage out of control in these dry forests that he wanted to avoid setting the trees on fire. But one of the cars, out on the open gravel driveway? Yeah, that would work. He picked the one farthest away from both the edge of the woods and the house.

Straightforward. Inelegant.

Described him pretty well, he thought.

He'd already duct-taped the bottle of lighter fluid to the half-full gas can, then taped a road flare to both of them. Redneck detonator. Keeping low to the ground, he crept out to the driveway, slid the bundle under the

SUV parked at the end of the row of cars, and lit the flare. Then he got the hell away, heading to the back side of the barn for shelter while keeping an eye on the house's front door.

Red sparks from the flare lit up the undercarriage in a weird glow, like the car was about to take off on a rocket engine. There was a hiss right before an air-breaking whump thundered, causing him instinctively to duck and turn away. He looked back up in time to see a wall of flame pour upward from the undercarriage, roaring as it engulfed the vehicle. A wave of heat washed past him, a hundred feet away. The SUV was on fire, crackling loud enough to fill the homestead.

As he hoped would happen, four or five guys poured out of the front of the house, shouting. Layne was there, staying back on the porch, hands to his head, shouting furious, panicked instructions. A couple of guys carrying semiautomatic pistols fanned out into the woods. Almost like they'd expected an attack. A couple of others went for the outdoor spigot and garden hoses to take care of the fire. No call to the fire department, Cormac was pretty sure, just like there'd been no call to the cops. He didn't want to draw any official attention to himself.

Cormac only had a few minutes to do this. Carefully and methodically, because rushing wouldn't do a bit of good, he went to the back of the house, trotted up the steps to a back porch and rickety door, which he opened slowly, waiting for hinges to squeak. He stepped inside, slowly closed the door behind him, without a sound. Layne most likely took Kuzniak's book to the house and set it down somewhere. Hell, the guy might even be reading it, to try to pick up where Kuzniak left off.

The inside was exactly what he'd expect from a bunch of bachelor types sharing a house. The place had an unwashed, dirty laundry odor to it. The door opened into a mudroom and kitchen. Beyond the kitchen doorway was a living room containing a worn sofa, armchairs, and a big LCD TV that was no doubt the most expensive, well-kept thing in the house. The kitchen smelled of burned coffee, but the rest of the place seemed to have been cleaned recently—the floor and surfaces weren't as grimy as he expected, even if dirty dishes filled the sink. He studied all the surfaces, imagining what Layne would have done when he came in, the first place he might have gone, where he'd have been likely to set the book. He hoped he wouldn't have to go looking upstairs for it.

He went down a hall along a threadbare runner on a hardwood floor, passed by the staircase—and found it there, lying on the sixth or so stair up, along with wallets and car keys and all the other detritus guys pulled out of their pockets when they came home. Exactly where Layne must have set it after walking in, because the sucker didn't know what he had, just wanted to keep it out of Cormac's hands. Fair enough. Cormac grabbed it—and paused when a creaking sounded on the stairs above him. He didn't give himself time to process the sound and what it meant, just slipped the book in his pocket and headed to the back door so he could get out of there before anyone had a chance to catch him.

The footsteps pounded down the stairs, chasing after him. Whoever it was had seen him, and he wasn't going to make it to the back door before they overtook him. He ducked into the kitchen to hide behind the wall, and waited.

The steps continued through the entrance way, and Cormac prepared to tackle whoever came into view. Legs braced, fists up.

It was Mollie.

The first thing he noticed, she had a semiautomatic in her hand, down by her leg, finger resting on the trigger guard. She was in a blue T-shirt and flannel pajama bottoms, her hair tied up with an elastic, makeup washed from her face. Her eyes widened when she spotted him, and he put his finger to his lips, a request for quiet. They stood like that a moment, and part of him figured he should maybe just knock her over and run like hell. But he didn't. He put his hands up, tried to project calm.

He hoped that wasn't her car he just blew up.

A whump and a whoosh blew from outside the front of the house, the fire spreading. Guys shouting for water, a fire extinguisher. Cormac had lingered here too long, and any second now someone was going to come in looking for that extinguisher. Mollie still didn't say anything. Didn't draw on him, either.

Gently, he put a hand on her shoulder, urged her aside so he could slip past her and through the doorway. Her expression turned quizzical, but he wasn't going to give himself away any more than he already had by answering her look. He nodded a thanks, backed away, and strode out the back door.

He kept expecting her to come after him, to yell at him to stop, for shots from her gun to ring out. None of that happened.

You are very lucky, Amelia thought at him as he continued down to the back of the property to slip over the barbed wire before Layne and his gang noticed.

Yeah, he figured he was.

AFTER A quick but careful trek through the woods, he returned to the Jeep and drove about thirty miles or so before stopping in a turnoff and taking a look at the notebook he'd gone through all that trouble for. Worst case, it would be in code, like Amy Scanlon's, and the wild goose chase would start all over again.

His luck was holding—the book wasn't in code.

The guy had sloppy handwriting and used a lot of abbreviations that needed interpreting, but once he got used to it he could read it okay. Not that any of it made much sense. There were recipes, diagrams, instructions, observations written in the form of experiments, like he was a chemist trying to come up with just the right formula. Mostly, Cormac let the contents flow through him, to Amelia.

He was a great experimenter, wasn't he? Amelia observed. *Definitely more of an alchemical magician than a folklorist or ceremonial ritualist, like Amy was. Definitely spent much time working on protection magic—I imagine that would be the most easily commodified skill to have if he was approaching people like Anderson Layne for work.*

Cormac sat back and let her read whatever she wanted, flipping back and forth, studying certain passages and referencing them with others. She kept up a running commentary, as if she were reading over his shoulder.

"So it was worth it?" he asked finally. "Burning up Layne's place to get this was worth it?"

I don't imagine you burned his entire *place. That fire would die down soon enough, I think. But yes, I do believe it was very much worth it. This is fascinating.*

"Then is it okay if we maybe hold off on the book club and get back home?" He turned the engine back on to encourage her.

Helpfully, she retreated from the fore and let him return the book to his pocket. They only had one set of eyes between them and couldn't read and drive at the same time.

They were back on the freeway when Amelia said, *Do you think Layne will attempt some kind of retribution for the attack?*

His original intent was that Layne wouldn't have any idea who'd done it and would even blame Nolan or some other faction. He didn't much care what war those guys got into. But Mollie—maybe she'd stay quiet. He didn't have any idea what their relationship was, if she was part of his operation, or if she just happened to be at the house at exactly the wrong time.

If she told Layne he'd broken into the house, he'd deal with it. But the worst case—she'd call the cops on him.

She wouldn't. Layne wouldn't let her. That would attract too much attention.

He really should have asked for her phone number back at the bar.

Chapter 19

AT THE apartment, Amelia referenced the books she had on hand, a small library she'd accumulated since they left prison and her own book of shadows that she was reconstructing from memory and recording in a hardcover-sized sketchbook. The handwriting varied between Cormac's crooked, unpracticed scrawl and a precise nineteenth-century cursive that he'd have expected to see on an old manuscript. They were both writing this book. It would confuse the hell out of anyone who tried to read it later.

It felt like homework to Cormac—he'd barely finished high school, mostly because Ben hauled him through their senior year by force of will. But Amelia was very excited by the whole thing.

Most of this I've seen before in one form or another, she announced in summary. *He seems to come from a Teutonic magical tradition, though he's cribbed quite a lot from the English—John Dee, Francis Bacon—as well. Some from the* Malleus Maleficarum, *and not the useful bits, alas. He's had teachers but doesn't name them, which makes a true tradition hard to identify. The second half of the thing is the most interesting. Do you know what I think?* He flipped through pages, reviewing some sections, looking at the book as a whole rather than in parts. *I think he may have copied much of this from the elder Kuzniak. I wonder if that's what put him on the path of learning about magic in the first place—finding his ancestor's magical history and wanting to know more.*

"So this is the jackpot—this ought to tell us how the first Kuzniak killed Crane."

I'm not sure, she murmured with a distracted air.

Cormac's eyes needed a break, even if Amelia didn't. He got a beer from the fridge and sat back to think.

I don't need to think, I need to read.

"Well, *I* need to think."

She kept talking, thinking out loud. If she'd had a body, she'd be pacing back and forth in front of him, her long skirt brushing the floor, her hands gesturing absently. He could almost see it. If they went to his imaginary meadow, he would.

There are several items I've not encountered before. The alchemical spell meant to draw gold out of the earth—the stories were right about that, the first Kuzniak did seem to be pursuing some kind of magi-

cal gold mining, though I can't say we've seen any evidence that such a method would actually work. *It's the old alchemist riddle, turning lead into gold. Such a nice idea, but can you imagine? It would hardly be worth it because if you could transform base metal into gold, even with a great deal of difficulty, you'd risk debasing the value of gold to such an extent the process wouldn't be worthwhile after all—you'd transform lead into gold and in so doing make gold just as valueless as lead.*

"You're rambling," Cormac stated.

Ah yes. Anyhow, I'd be curious to review his findings and perhaps experiment, see if such a thing could be accomplished.

Now that would be interesting. They wouldn't have to produce enough to debase gold. Just enough to keep from having to find another job, right?

I've just had a thought—what if this is really the magic Judi and Frida are looking for, and they're not interested at all in how Kuzniak killed Crane?

And the two old ladies weren't about to try to go after Kuzniak and Layne and that pack of thugs. But Cormac shows up on their doorstep, and suddenly they have a way in. "And they'd trust that we would just hand something like that over?"

Perhaps not. Oh, and look at this—he mentions another curious item—an amulet with protective properties. Something he must have inherited from his great-grandfather, along with scraps of other magical knowledge. It's noteworthy because he says he isn't sure how it works. Obviously I can't tell anything about it because it isn't here. He must have stored it somewhere else. We should have examined him more thoroughly—

"Rifled through the pockets of a dead man, you mean?"

That's putting it rather crudely.

"It's all odds and ends. I thought we were trying to solve a hundred-year-old murder."

Well, now we're also trying to mine for gold—

His phone rang from inside the pocket of his jacket where he'd left it. Setting the beer aside, hauling himself to where he'd hung the jacket over a chair, he retrieved the phone, checked caller ID—Anderson Layne. He supposed that was only a matter of time.

You probably shouldn't answer—

He clicked the answer button. "Yeah?"

"You must think you're pretty tough, don't you?" The guy was trying hard to sound casual, amused, but the edge to his voice revealed anger. Maybe even fear. So Mollie told Layne. Cormac couldn't get too upset at her—she didn't owe him anything. Or maybe Layne just figured it out.

"Kuzniak's protection spells didn't outlast him, did they?" he replied conversationally.

"I'm starting to think you're the one who killed Kuzniak, if you wanted his book that bad."

That didn't make any sense. "You want to know who killed him, look at your own gang. You're the ones messing with all this magic without knowing what the hell you're doing. What did Kuzniak tell you, that he knew how to suck gold out of those rocks? You think just because vampires are real, something like that'll work?"

The pause lasted long enough Cormac wondered what kind of nerve he hit with that one. What was it statistics said, most murders were committed by someone the victim knew? Crimes of passion? Maybe Kuzniak had been killed by his own magic backfiring. . . .

Intriguing, Amelia observed. *But not so simple. Why would such a thing happen? How?*

Layne was feigning calm. "Why don't we talk about this, Bennett? Come back down, we'll have a civilized conversation."

"Not likely."

"Then I'll meet you somewhere. Pick a spot. Anywhere."

"Not interested."

"Bennett, just a minute now, don't think you can just walk away—"

He hung up and tossed the phone on the nightstand.

Amelia waited a long time before asking, *Should we be worried?*

Oh, probably, he thought. Not that he was going to lose sleep over it. "Let's find out if Kuzniak really knew how to dig for gold."

FIRST, THEY needed to find a spot that was likely to have gold. Fortunately, a number of gold mines, both defunct and still operating, were within reasonable distance. Cormac picked a spot near Cripple Creek, which had been an active gold mining area for over a century, and wasn't in such a remote mountain location that he'd have trouble getting there in the middle of winter.

Kuzniak wasn't polite enough to provide a finished, fully working spell in his book. Magicians rarely did—they wrote in code, like Amy Scanlon did; they left bits out so the book would be useless without them, leaving others to piece the clues together. And maybe blow themselves up in the process. This meant Amelia had to reconstruct his research, adding her own knowledge to come up with something that seemed reasonable. As reasonable as any of this was. The elements of the spell she constructed didn't surprise Cormac—the major elements of most European-derived magic tended to be the same; the details changed depending on what you were trying to do.

They'd done this enough over the last couple of years, it was familiar. He could even work some of these spells himself, without her help. He'd rather not, though. Magic still felt like cheating.

She wanted to work the spell at midnight, of course. Gathering the right materials took a few days. He would never get used to walking into the fancy cooking stores for the various hard-to-get herbs she needed. Made him feel like a buffalo in a church. Finding unscented candles was another challenge he never thought he'd have to face. Colors were fine, colors could be useful as elements in various spells. But since meeting Amelia, he'd spent way too much time standing in front of walls of candles labeled with names like "Cranberry Spice" and "Warm Honey." Christian bookstores and other religious supply shops became their go-to spots to find simple, unadorned, non-scented votive candles. Another deep irony, he observed. If only those kind, wide-eyed women at the cash registers knew what those candles were being used for.

Following Amelia's instructions on what to pack, he loaded up the Jeep and headed out at dusk.

The nocturnal lifestyle he'd been leading lately felt familiar, even comforting. This was what he'd done for years: stay in for most of the day and earn his living at night. Driving south, watching the sun set over the mountains—he'd done this all before. Times like this, he felt like he was in the right place, that he fit. He was calm.

He hiked for a time, double-checked the GPS and cross-referenced with some historical maps he'd researched. In this creek valley, a dozen claims had been staked and four of them had turned into working gold mines. One of those had produced right up into the 1970s. They hadn't been abandoned because they were paid out. Rather, the effort to get what ore remained—and transport it, process it, refine it, and so on—was no longer cost effective. There ought to be gold here still, and if it could be gotten with magic, they'd get it.

Here. This is a good spot. Amelia stopped him in a flattened clearing, south-facing and clear of snow. The moonlight was faint, and he used a flashlight to see by. He set down her pack of gear and waited for her instructions.

She had what she called a cauldron. It was really a small cast-iron pot, a highly portable fire pit maybe eight inches across. His dad might have used something like this to cook supper Dutch-oven style over a fire. It was a convenient way to create light and heat for rituals. Charcoal briquettes lined the bottom of it for fuel. He set this up, lit the charcoal, got it burning. She set up another little dish with a few ingredients and supplies, including a gold band he'd picked up at a pawn shop.

Like seeks like, she explained. *You must start with some gold in order to call gold to you.*

It made a weird kind of sense. The rest of the spell she'd found in Kuzniak's notebook she wasn't so sure about.

All right. To begin, we must strip. Divest yourself of your clothing, please.

Times like this he wished she was standing in front of him so he could glare at her. "You know it's the middle of winter. It's fucking cold out here."

I assure you, there's a very good reason for it. A ritual like this must begin with a cleansing, to shed any negative energies and ill feeling.

"Yeah? You want to talk about ill feeling, do you?"

It isn't so terribly cold, is it?

It was. His balls were very certain it was. "You haven't been cold in a hundred years, you don't know what you're talking about."

You're not scared, are you?

"No. But I'm as pure as I'm ever going to get, with or without my clothes."

Please, Cormac. Only for a few minutes . . .

"I suppose I can tell myself you like seeing me naked."

She had nothing to say to that, which made him smirk. If she'd had a body, he'd bet she'd be blushing. He shrugged off his jacket, peeled off his shirt. Boots, jeans, boxers. And yes, it was cold. He didn't mind so much in his clothes, but he sure felt it now in the sensitive bits. He was going to get her for this. . . .

"I hope you're feeling this," he muttered.

It is . . . rather unpleasant.

"Let's get this over with."

He gathered that in other circumstances this might involve a full-on bath, but since there were no enchanted springs nearby, they were left using a washcloth and bottle of water. Damp cloth on the skin, freezing air—not a good combination, and she wouldn't let him hurry.

Finally, she deemed them pure enough in body and intentions to proceed, and he quickly slipped back into his clothes, leaving the jacket aside for now.

The spell she'd concocted was based on sympathies, she explained. Certain herbs had a connection to the earth, certain stones or crystals aligned certain energies, all of which would call to the gold in the earth. She thought the spell was supposed to turn it liquid, and it would bubble to the surface, where it would collect in pools they could simply gather up. It would be impressive, if it worked.

Guided by her instructions, he drew a circle in powdered chalk. Drew the appropriate symbols at the cardinal points, all familiar actions. Placed the gold ring at the center of the circle. The fire in the iron pot was burning low but steadily. A sequence of dried herbs tossed on the coals produced a heady incense.

Here in the dark, in a halo of orange light, Amelia murmuring in the back of his head, pungent smoke surrounding him, he did feel as if he slipped out of the world and into a sideways one, where anything could happen. The earth under him might crack open, spirits might fly down from heaven.

Shaking his head, he woke himself from whatever trance was weaving through him.

There, she murmured, which meant . . . was it done?

They waited.

The coals burned down; the chill returned to their circle of warmth. Nothing else happened, no cracks breaking in the soil, no veins of ore rising to the surface, no liquid threads pooling. They were both patient. Cormac sat still until he started shivering and had to go put on his jacket.

I'm not entirely sure what to expect, Amelia said, sounding perplexed. *I should try again, make adjustments. Hope for the best.*

This was going to be a long night.

Chapter 20

AMELIA REMEMBERED the very last time she spoke with her brother. With anyone in her family, really. She had already told her mother and father she wanted to leave. To travel in order to pursue her education was what she'd told them, with a safe-sounding plan to go to Paris and stay with respectable friends, never mind that she'd almost immediately leave for less safe and less respectable destinations around the world. This was perhaps not her wisest course of action—her mother still broke into uncontrollable weeping whenever anyone mentioned Arthur Pembroke, whom Amelia had so indecorously refused. Refusing a good offer of marriage was one thing. Wishing to travel was ever so much worse, apparently. But she'd told them, set them off weeping again. At least, her mother wept and her father glared at her, his soft face growing more florid by the second.

They demanded that she speak with James. She gathered he'd been ordered to "knock some sense into the silly girl." Figuratively, of course, but the level of outrage she'd generated might indicate otherwise.

He arrived later that afternoon by carriage. She was in the garden reading a book and had to be summoned to the drawing room, which seemed to infuriate him, as if she should have been waiting for him, dutiful and quiet, hands folded in her lap. As if she should spend her whole life waiting, never speaking a word.

She arrived in the drawing room. He was pacing back and forth before the fireplace, agitated, like a character out of an Austen novel. She stood, trying to think of what to say. To speak exactly the right words so he would understand. Her mind was a blank.

"Are you insane? Really, Amelia. Are you utterly out of your mind?" He turned on her with a look he might give a hound with no house training. He was a handsome man, tall and fit, very well dressed by a London tailor, hair and mustache trimmed by his well-trained valet.

"I hadn't thought so," she said softly. "I simply don't think I can stay here with you all giving me that *look*." She felt smaller and smaller, regressing in time and space, until she might have been a child again. "My plans are not so very strange—"

"And what exactly do you imagine people will think of us? How will your *plans* reflect on the family, do you think?"

Truthfully, she didn't care. The family could take care of itself. It didn't need her. She was tired of this, though. Tired of James, tired of all the shouting and the tears, tired of disappointing everyone so thoroughly. She wanted to be *gone.* James could rant all he wanted, she put her mind elsewhere, repeating to herself the Latin names of plants with medicinal properties. *Salix alba, Stachys byzantina . . .*

"Amelia!" His shout echoed.

Startled, she flinched and looked up at him. He'd crossed the room to stand directly in front of her. She was too surprised to back away.

"What in God's name do you want!" He said it as a curse, not a question, but she answered anyway.

"I want to find fairies."

She'd never said it out loud before. It sounded stark, desperate, childish. Nevertheless, it was as true as it had ever been. Hands clasped tightly together, a heavy lump in her belly, she waited for his response.

He laughed. If he had done anything else, said any words at all, she might have stayed. If they could have had any conversation at all, if he had asked for explanation, if he had listened—she might have stayed. But he laughed.

She turned and left the room. Her one bag was already packed, she had saved a good deal of cash, and in the future she would have access through banks to her inheritance, which came through one of her grandmothers and the rest of the family could not touch. It was her one stroke of luck. She would walk all the way to the village to catch the train. She would never return.

But she did, so many years later, in such an altered form. She wished she could talk to James just one more time. She wished he would say something to her without shouting.

Now, she had Cormac, who never shouted. More than that, he *listened*. She could weep.

A COUPLE of hours before dawn, she gave up. Cormac collected what was left of the tools and materials and crawled into the Jeep to put his head back and catch an hour or two of sleep.

Amelia didn't want to sleep. *Perhaps if we perform the spell on the night of a full moon—*

He shook his head. "You know I don't like to spend full moon nights running all over hell and back."

Surely Kitty and Ben can do without you for one night.

The couple didn't know it, but Cormac liked to stay close to town on full moon nights, when their wolf sides took charge, forcing them to shape-shift. They usually went with their pack into the mountains or out east into the remote plains, far away from civilization and trouble. They'd been doing it long enough, they could handle themselves just fine. They'd been just fine without him when he was in prison. But now that he was out, Cormac liked to be within easy reach. They'd never called for help. Not yet. But just in case. "No."

Then we find someplace near Denver with gold in the rocks. This shouldn't be hard.

"Are you sure it's even possible?" She didn't say anything, which meant she had doubts. "You know that's the trouble those old alchemists had—if you don't know something's impossible, you'll keep trying until you kill yourself."

I will not kill myself. I haven't yet. Cormac, come talk to me in person. So to speak.

This was the woman who had survived her own execution. Cormac shouldn't even try arguing with her. He let his mind fall into their shared space, the high country meadow.

Here, the sun was setting, casting a late-day glow over the valley, the pattern of clouds and light much like the sunset they had watched the previous evening. The sight gave him a jolt, throwing his sense of time off balance. Time of day, weather—it seemed arbitrary here, when it shouldn't, because he decided what happened here. Didn't he?

"The sunset last night," Amelia said. "You were calm. You latched onto the sense of calm."

He was sitting on his usual rock; she was standing nearby, looking into the western sky. He guessed she was right. Dealing with his mental state would be easier if he didn't feel like his brain was working all by itself so much of the time.

"I'd be even more calm if you'd let me sleep."

She came toward him, eyes lit with enthusiasm. "So many variables are involved in a spell like this, it could take months to test them all. *Years,* even. Performing the spell at midnight locally is a safe choice, of course. But does the phase of the moon play a part, or the time of the year? Both? This might be a spell that can only be performed once in decades, if an alignment of the phase of the moon and planets and one of the solstices or equinoxes is a factor—"

"I don't want to spend years doing this."

"Well no, of course not, since we don't even know if this spell is possible. I'm merely reviewing possibilities. The more I review them, the more I think it can't work. It's just as you say, the old alchemy problem, which as it turned out didn't need magic to solve, but modern chemical manipulation. Kuzniak wrote down plenty of speculation, but I gather he did very little practical testing. It's less an idea than it is a rumor."

"Question is," Cormac said, "does Layne know it

doesn't work? Layne knows I wanted that book—I'm sure he thinks I'm going to go after the gold. Like he did, like Kuzniak did. Why else would I want it?"

"Does that matter?"

"Yeah. It means he isn't going to leave me alone."

"Cormac, I'd like to try one more thing, if you agree to it. I'd like to send a message."

"What message? To who?"

"To the person who wrote to us about Amy Scanlon," she said, carefully, as if she expected an argument.

Interesting idea. If this person knew about Amy, he knew about magic. It was a long shot, but Cormac was happy enough to light that fuse to see what happened.

Back in the world, eyes open, Amelia typed out the e-mail. "If you know of Amy Scanlon, then you must know something of magic. Perhaps even a great deal. If this is so, I'd like to get your opinion on a situation I've encountered. I have information on the possibility of a spell that produces gold, presumably by pulling it directly from the rock without the effort of mining it. It seems to be a sympathetic-based ritual with earth-element components designed to draw forth the desired effect—" and so on.

Her discussion of magic made it sound scientific rather than mystical. She didn't have any agenda besides just figuring this stuff out, which meant she didn't need to dress it up in mysticism to impress anyone. She didn't write what she'd learned in any kind of code, because she wasn't competing with anyone. Her curiosity was fierce and genuine.

Sometimes, Cormac thought about the kind of magician he might have ended up with living inside his head. Someone determined to control absolutely, who might have broken him without thinking twice. Amelia had tried to break her way in, until she found that negotiating worked better. But say it had been Roman whose spirit was locked in the stones of the prison—Cormac might not have survived. Or worse, he might have survived but been trapped, overcome, crushed by magic and intention, fighting a constant battle just to maintain his self. His whole life co-opted. Would anyone—Ben, Kitty—even have noticed?

Better not to think of it.

She finished writing, read it half a dozen times, still wasn't fully satisfied but he convinced her it was good enough, so he sent it. Then spent a full minute staring at the screen, waiting for a response that he rationally knew wasn't likely to show up immediately. He started to shut off the computer.

Just a little longer. An answer could come any second.

"I'm not going to sit around here waiting."

But—

He shut it down anyway and grabbed his jacket and keys. Best thing to do was to take a walk. Burn off some of the impatience.

Chapter 21

HE ARRIVED at New Moon, sure that Kitty and Ben would be there. That was always his excuse. It wasn't like he *needed* to go out; he'd never go out at all, if not for meeting those two at their restaurant. Maybe an exaggeration, maybe not. Sometimes they weren't there; he'd go anyway, sit in the back and read a book and have a beer before packing up and going home. But odds were good they'd be there, and he could give them an update on what he'd found. Leaving out the exploding bits, of course.

He went in, paused a moment to take in the shape of the place, the number of people and where they were sitting, the traffic patterns, the mood. This was a mellow after-work crowd, carrying with it an atmosphere both exhausted and giddy. Shaun, working behind the bar tonight, gave Cormac a cautious nod in greeting.

"Kitty here?" Cormac asked.

"She should be here in half an hour or so," the bartender said. "You want something to drink or are you just dropping by?"

"Sure. The usual." Predictable. He'd become painfully predictable. He had a usual watering hole where people recognized him and they knew what he drank without asking.

And why not? You're practically middle-aged, you ought to be more settled than you were in your youth.

He was *not* going to start thinking about that.

Shaun finished pouring the beer and set it on the bar. "Thanks," Cormac muttered, and carried it to a table in back, where he could sit in a corner and watch. And read—at Amelia's insistence, he brought along Milo Kuzniak's notebook. He sat, drank his beer, read, and didn't much care how it looked from the outside.

Sure enough, Kitty came in about a half an hour later. Ben was with her, and the two were talking. Or she was talking, and he had a vaguely amused smile on while he nodded at her encouragingly. They spotted him quickly, as soon as the door opened. They could smell him.

The ensuing pattern was familiar: she checked in with her pack members, Shaun at the bar and anyone else who happened to be around. She had the friendly, amiable disposition of a politician without the artifice, handing out friendly touches and comforting smiles. Her pack members, the other werewolves, leaned into her, following her with devoted gazes. Cormac wasn't sure she realized the effect she had on them. She'd say she was just being nice.

Ben came straight over and took the chair across from Cormac. "Well?"

"Well what?"

He shrugged, leaving Cormac wide open to stick his foot in his mouth. Kitty rescued him by sweeping over, setting two mugs of beer on the table, and perching in the other chair. She revealed the book she'd held tucked under her arm and pushed it across the table to him.

"Look what I got. Galleys for the new book. Isn't it pretty?"

On top of everything else she managed, she was an author. That was more of a sideline to the talk radio show, but if she was going to be doing all that talking anyway, might as well write some of it down.

It was a cheap paperback, not the final fancy hardcover that would be out in a few months. *Storytellers: Myth and History,* the title read. The cover was a photograph, her portrait against a backdrop of pine trees. She was all made up and airbrushed and looked like a celebrity, which he supposed was the idea. But it didn't look like the Kitty he knew.

"Congratulations," he said, his tone as even as ever.

"Thanks! This is an extra. You know, if you wanted to read it. Or something." She blinked hopefully.

He was about to politely decline, but Amelia insisted. *Yes, we want to read it.* He picked up the copy, and Kitty beamed.

"You find out anything new?" Ben asked. "I assume that's why you're here."

"Don't think I just stopped by for a beer and company?"

"Not that you'd ever admit it," Ben observed, which was more accurate than not.

"So what have you found?" Kitty demanded.

He started to say something, stopped. Thought for a second about how to condense everything that had happened since the run-in with Nolan and Eddie. Realized that Ben would ask how much of what he'd been doing was technically illegal, and Cormac didn't precisely know. He didn't *think* they were trespassing on private land when they experimented with that mining spell. Bottom line, none of it would make Ben and Kitty happy, and he didn't want the grilling he'd go through if his answer was too vague.

They watched him expectantly, waiting for an answer.

He said, "I got a hit on the stuff we posted online. Don't know if anything'll come of it. But it may be another lead." It all depended on whether or not they had e-mail waiting for them when they got home.

"Yeah?" Kitty asked. "What kind of a hit?"

"Hard to tell. Someone who knows about Amy. And who knows about Kumarbis."

Kitty sat forward at that—a wolf on the scent, ears up and nose quivering. "Knows how? This person—they must be a vampire, to know about Kumarbis. What would a vampire know about Amy's book—"

"I told you, I don't know. We've just exchanged a couple of e-mails so far. I'm still feeling the person out."

She sighed, obviously disappointed. "If you find out anything more, and if you think we can even trust them, find out what they know about Roman, the Long Game, all of it."

"Yeah. One step at a time."

"Thank you again," Kitty said. "For working on all this."

He brushed her off out of habit. "I figure I'm in it as deep as you are at this point."

Can you please finish your beer so we can go see if our mysterious correspondent has answered?

How could someone who was functionally dead be that impatient?

Kitty rambled on about the new book, the release schedule, and possibly going on a signing tour, which gave him a twinge of anxiety. Traveling all over the country meeting total strangers—what could possibly go wrong? He nursed his beer and listened to his friends' banter.

The phone in his pocket rang. He considered not answering, then thought it might be Layne wanting to blow off more steam. Curious, he checked, while Ben and Kitty looked on with interest. Because they were nosy.

The caller ID wasn't Layne this time. He answered and heard, "Cormac?" It was Mollie.

He got up from the table and walked a few paces off, then realized that wouldn't be far enough away to keep the couple and their werewolf ears from listening in, so he went out the front door. Aware the whole time that Ben was smirking and Kitty's eyebrows had lifted—they knew his caller was female.

"Hey," he answered the phone, propping himself up against the brick wall outside the door.

"Hi. Andy gave me your number." She didn't sound happy, and Cormac braced. She waited, and waited. Expectantly.

He said, innocently as he could, which wasn't very, "Heard you guys had a fire out at the ranch."

"I should have shot you where you stood, Cormac Bennett. That was my car you blew up."

He winced. Just his luck. "Well. Thank you for not shooting me."

"You're lucky Andy won't let me call the cops. He won't even let me call my insurance company, because *they'd* call the cops."

He wasn't going to apologize. He refused to apologize. He'd do it all over again. He'd just pick a different car. "What's he expect you to do?"

"I made Andy give me his car. And five grand."

"That was big of him."

"I suppose I deserve it, hanging out with him in the first place. I don't know what all he gets up to, I don't want to. But God, Cormac, what the hell!"

"I needed a distraction."

"I know better than to ask Andy what he's doing, but you—you all but vanish for twenty years, then show up setting cars on fire? He says you're some kind of magical vampire hunter—is that true?"

She didn't know the stories. Didn't know about his father, had stayed out of the politics of what followed while she was off getting married and having kids.

"Mollie, it's a lot like the stuff with Layne, you really don't want to know."

There was a pause, and he could just about picture her straightening, brushing back her hair, and changing her stance in order to change her voice. Because the next thing she said was gentle, suggestive. "Cormac, I know it's been a long time. I don't know what you have going on in your life right now. But I was thinking maybe we could get together. Catch up, you know? I could bore you with pictures of my kids."

He didn't know if it was the sudden shift in the tone

of her voice or his natural suspicion, but he didn't trust the request. "Layne put you up to this, didn't he? He's sitting right there, isn't he?"

A sigh. He imagined her looking across whatever room she was in to her brother egging her on. And to think, for a split second Cormac thought maybe she really wanted to see him.

"He wants to meet. Just to talk."

"I bet he does. The answer's still no, not as long as he's likely to put a bullet in me."

"He was working with that Kuzniak jerk so he wouldn't have to put bullets in anyone! Just watch them keel over dead when they get in his way!"

"Like Kuzniak," Cormac said.

A long silence followed. Amelia murmured, *Anderson Layne found something. He discovered something.*

They were supposed to be washing their hands of it.

"Cormac—"

"Mollie. It really has been good to see you. I have to go." He hung up. Sighed. Well, at least he had her number now.

You wanted to ask her out for drinks.

It wouldn't work out, he thought. He wasn't that kind of guy.

He could just go on home, but Kitty or Ben—or both—would call and demand to know what was happening. Best get it over with now, in person, when they might actually believe he wasn't hiding something. He went back inside.

They were waiting for him, and they didn't even have to ask, just looked at him with these expectant, questioning gazes. Puppy dog eyes? Hm.

"What was that all about?" Kitty finally asked when he didn't say anything.

"Just a call. Not important," he said.

"You were out there a long time," Kitty said. She might have batted her eyelashes.

"Yeah?" He found some beer left in his mug and drank it down.

Kitty added, "Is she nice?"

He rolled his eyes. "I should get going. I've still got some work to do. Let you guys have your fun in peace."

"You'll let us know if anything comes up?" Ben said.

"Always do."

"Not likely," he said, his smile friendly enough, but the dig was there as well. The words held a lot of shared history. A lot of not talking.

"If it's important, I'll let you know," he amended and waved himself out.

Chapter 22

HE'D JUST unlocked the apartment's front door when Amelia demanded, *The laptop. Turn on the laptop. My God, why do these things take so long, we should have just left it on. . . .*

He took his time getting inside, closing the door behind him, setting the dead bolt, turning on the lights, heading to the kitchenette for a glass of water—

Cormac!

Then, he turned on the computer.

New e-mail was waiting for them.

"A new take on the alchemical prize. Interesting. I have studied and practiced magic for many years, and everyone seems to think they have a way to make gold out of something else. The closest I've come to what you're suggesting—mining gold magically, pulling it out of the ground without use of chemicals or equipment—are various earthmoving spells. Spells to move stone, rituals to cause earthquakes. One could build a mine using such magical techniques. But any gold ore would still need to be physically mined. Unless you've discovered evidence to the contrary?"

Amelia couldn't wait to start typing a reply. Her urgency felt like a throbbing running down his arms to his fingers.

"You never had a pen pal, did you?" he said.

I had correspondences all my life, with some of the most diligent arcane scholars of my day. All the letters I collected—I've lost them all, along with my other artifacts and treasures. But I would have to wait weeks for replies to my letters. Days at the very least. This—this is nearly instantaneous. You have no idea the technologies you take for granted.

"No doubt." He thought about his cell phone and how it meant he could never really disappear. Not unless he just left it behind and drove off into the sunset. He'd thought about doing that.

He let Amelia type. "No, I have no evidence, only rambling notes and speculation. I've started experimenting, but I'm not hopeful. You've confirmed my fears. The idea was simply so intriguing I could not pass over it without giving it at least some thought."

She sent the message, stared at the screen, and he imagined her rubbing her hands together in anticipation. Their correspondent might reply immediately.

Or they could be waiting all night. Cormac thought he might as well go to sleep—if Amelia would let him.

But they didn't have to wait that long. The program pinged incoming e-mail; their correspondent was online.

He'd written: "The path of magic is never clear cut. I commend your curiosity and your dedication. Have you learned anything new about breaking Amy Scanlon's code?"

"Several leads. Nothing definite, I'm afraid. My guess is she used a personal, shifting code, something that only had meaning to her. If we knew the key, we could find the pattern. But I didn't know her personally and I couldn't guess what she might have used."

Again, a quick response: "Does she have any family, any close friends still living?"

They hesitated in their response. So far, they hadn't exchanged details. No names but Amy's, no locations. Only generalizations, abstractions. Cormac was leery about giving too much away. They had little enough as it was. "That's one of the leads I'm following. Nothing definite, yet."

"What do you hope to find in this book of shadows when you are able to read it?"

"Your confidence that I will is heartening. I have some questions that need answering; her book of shadows seems likely to contain such answers."

"What kind of questions?"

Cormac suddenly had the feeling of being interrogated and drew his hands back from the keyboard.

Amelia argued, *If Kitty is right, and knowing about Kumarbis means this person is a vampire, he might have some insight into the Long Game. We could ask—*

"I don't want to show our hand," Cormac said. "I don't want to give away who we are. We start talking about the Long Game, who knows what'll come up. This is about the book for now. That's it."

Your paranoia has served you well in the past. I suppose I can't argue with you now.

That was probably giving him more credit than he deserved. Now, how to be cagey without entirely shutting down the line of communication? This was the kind of thing Kitty was good at.

"Historical magic," Amelia typed, using Cormac's hands. The answer was both true and disingenuous. "Spells that might have been lost to time. My understanding is that Amy Scanlon was interested in the past. For example—you yourself mentioned the possibility of creating earthquakes by magical means; have you actually done this, or seen it done? Or is it only in stories? Mere rumor." According to Kitty, Amy must have had some kind of earthmoving spell to be able to cause the cave-in at the mine there at the end. Maybe it was in the book's coded sections.

"I never like to say *mere* rumor. But I will say this: I have good reason to believe that the eruption of Vesuvius that buried Pompeii was instigated by magic. The volcano was naturally ready to erupt, of course—but the ultimate trigger was not natural."

"Good heavens," Amelia wrote, both honest reaction and conversational filler. "That's extraordinary. That raises so many questions, doesn't it?"

"Yes, but I don't believe that's the problem you're working on, is it?"

Amelia's mind had gone off in a dozen different directions, to other natural disasters that might have been caused by magic, to the reasons someone might have wanted to cause Vesuvius to erupt—revenge against the city? An overblown assassination attempt? An accident? Cormac pulled her back to the conversation at hand.

Amelia replied, "I'm currently investigating two deaths. At least one of them involved a duel between two men known to use magic. In both cases, men known to be powerful magicians were struck dead with no evidence of being attacked, injured, or any usual offensive magic being used against them."

The next reply didn't come immediately. Cormac went to the fridge for a beer, took his time crossing the four feet back to the table, while Amelia seethed with impatience.

An answer waited: "In magical duels, the magician who wins is often not the one with the most powerful offense, but the one with the strongest defense. Look to see how their opponents were shielded. My apologies, I have to go now, but I'm sure we'll talk again. I look forward to our next exchange."

A defense strong enough to kill. Wasn't unheard of. Thoughtful, Cormac leaned back in his chair.

This person is brilliant, Amelia said, gushing. *I wonder who he is? Or she? My goodness, I think I'm blushing.*

He refrained from asking how she could blush without a body. "You ask who he is, we'll have to tell who we are."

Not necessarily. But if we lie to him about who we are, then there's no reason to believe he'll tell the truth about who he is. Oh, this anonymity is so useful, but terribly frustrating, isn't it? I'll have to look into using my scrying spells, but who knows if they'll even work on e-mail. Though I did know someone who attempted to cast spells via telegraph, as an experiment. With ambiguous results, unfortunately, but I wonder if the technique could be adapted.

He decided it was time to go to bed, before she went off on another research jag. Maybe she'd even stop talking long enough for him to actually fall asleep.

I'm not that bad.

He didn't credit that with an answer.

* * *

He lay in bed for a long time the next morning, thinking.

Again, he was in the meadow, and Amelia was again pacing. Cormac wondered if he could lean up against a nearby tree trunk, close his eyes, and go to sleep inside the half-dreaming world of their minds. He hadn't slept well, waking up every hour or so with some new thought, Amelia probing him with some conjecture about Kuzniak, Crane, the other Kuzniak, and how they were all connected. He thought it could wait until morning; she didn't. Finally, he'd given in. But he still wanted to sleep.

"If Kuzniak killed Crane in the manner the stories about it say, the evidence of it ought to be in his book. But there's nothing!"

"It's not a very thorough book."

"Yes, I've seen that. If the young Milo learned all his magic from it, it's no wonder he ended up dead. There must be another book. Another source from which he acquired his knowledge. *Something.*"

"Or we've missed something," Cormac said.

"I haven't missed anything, I don't *miss* things."

Amelia had studied the book over and over. She'd deciphered the handwriting, figured out abbreviations, copied the whole thing into her own book. Cormac agreed, she probably hadn't missed anything.

Then the solution wasn't in the writing. He sat up.

Amelia came toward him. "Cormac, what is it?

You've thought of something, I can see the look in your eyes—"

He shook his head, shook away the meadow, and sat up in bed, swinging his legs to the floor. Sun came in through the cheap blinds, casting light over the clutter in the place that was so much easier to ignore at night.

Kuzniak's book was in the lockbox where Amelia kept the most valuable—or dangerous—of the artifacts they'd collected. He went to get it off the set of makeshift shelves on the far wall, pulled it out, ignored her when she complained that he left the box open. Sat back and flipped through it, looking at everything but the writing. Feeling along the pages, the spine, the covers; holding the pages up to the light, up to his nose. Smelled like paper. A little bit musty, like an attic.

He found it in the very back, between the last page and the back cover. The last few pages of the thing were blank, like Kuzniak hadn't had a chance to fill them all, so they hadn't gotten this far in their reading. He held the inside back cover to the light, ran his thumb over it, and found the imprint—the shape of a Maltese cross a couple of inches wide, pressed into the endpapers. Once upon a time, someone had stored something here, enclosed inside the book.

"Look at that," he murmured, knowing full well that Amelia was seeing everything he did. The shape had an irregularity at the top, maybe a ring, but there didn't seem to be a chain running through it. It looked like a piece of jewelry, some kind of metal pendant or amulet. And it had to have been kept in here a long time to make this kind of an imprint.

Then where is it now?

"Good question. If there was some kind of spell attached to it, it would have survived Kuzniak's death, wouldn't it?"

That's the whole point of amulets and charms, to lock the magic in place so you can give it to someone else, so the magic will survive them. This thing might be very much older than Kuzniak. Either of them.

"And what's it do?"

It kills people, I'd wager.

He frowned. "Great. Want to bet that Layne has it now?" And did he know what he had . . . ?

Cormac, I want to talk. Face-to-face.

Sighing, he propped himself against the wall, leaned his head back, closed his eyes. Put himself in the meadow, and found Amelia by his side. He almost expected to see a copy of the book in her hand—if she'd really memorized it, she'd be able to do that, manifest a copy in their imaginations. But it was just her, and she was alight with urgency.

"We can solve this, work out *exactly* what happened. Put yourself in Kuzniak's place," Amelia said.

"Older or younger?"

"Younger. The great-grandson. If we know what happened to him, we'll know what happened to Augustus Crane, and we can go back to Judi and be done with this whole sorry business."

Right. He could make some guesses. Milo Kuzniak the younger probably had a similar background and upbringing to Cormac's. Native Colorado, a rural family with deep roots in the region. Ranchers or farmers, or maybe even mining or some other local industry. Maybe a connection to the militia and sovereignty movements, which would be how he hooked up with Layne. This guy would even have had a connection to the supernatural, same as Cormac's family. Only instead of being hunters, they were magicians. Maybe not seriously—it might have just been stories, at least until Kuzniak got ahold of his great-grandfather's book. Family might have kept it as an heirloom, or maybe it had been stuck in some trunk in an attic, but Kuzniak would have latched onto it and seen it as something more. That would have started him down the path—with some people, it didn't take much. He'd have studied what little his great-grandfather knew, added his own discoveries. And then gone to work for the people he knew in his own neck of the woods.

Maybe pacing wasn't such a bad idea. He stood, to

wake himself up, to get his brain working. "The cross tucked in the book. Would he have known what it was?"

"He might not have known what was, or what it did. The book never mentions it, apart from discussing amulets in general."

"But he'd have known it did *something* and kept it with him. Could it have killed him?"

She seemed to fold into her own world when she was thinking hard, tugging at her ear and staring off into space, pacing through the grass and absently swishing her skirt out of the way when it snagged on something. He imagined this was exactly how she looked when she was alive, in a Victorian parlor or on the streets of some ornate European city.

She said, "He might never have taken it out of the book. But it wasn't with the book when he died, was it? You searched him—it wasn't in any of his other pockets, was it? Could he have hidden it about his person? Then where is it now? Did it remain with him? Is it wherever Layne put the body?"

That didn't feel right to Cormac. Layne would have searched the body before getting rid of it, even if it was just to pull loose change out of the guy's pockets.

He spoke slowly, arranging his thoughts while he did. "What if . . . maybe he didn't know what exactly it did, but he used it to give himself some kind of credibility. Said it was powerful, bragged about it to Layne."

"And then gave it to Layne as a sign of goodwill? Or Layne took it, as a pledge of loyalty? He wanted magic but didn't trust Kuzniak." She stopped, turned to face him, her eyes wide.

Cormac added, "Kuzniak tries to get it back—and sure enough, Layne's got all the power now and kills him instead. Whatever it is, whatever it does—it killed him." Even sounded like a wizards' duel—a rivalry turned into a fight for power, and *bang,* it's done. "He freaks out, calls us—then figured out what happened. And now he thinks he's got all the magic. And he wants to meet with me. He won't even need bullets."

"I'm desperate to get my hands on that thing," Amelia said.

Her eyes were wide, gleaming, and she reached for him—he was standing right there, and she took hold of his hands, clutching them in excitement, and he squeezed back before even thinking. For a moment, they both went still, uncertain. He didn't pull away; neither did she. It was like they were both waiting for the other to make a move. And so they remained still, frozen in contact. As close as they had been for the last few years, living mind to mind, inseparable, he couldn't remember feeling this *close* to her. He could feel the pressure in her hands, warmth in her skin, which shouldn't have been possible because she didn't exist, not really. She was dead—but that didn't matter here. He took a step in, brushed his thumb along her chin and yes, it felt like skin, impossibly soft. Reflexively, she tipped her chin back, looking up at him. It would take so little effort to lean into her, to bring his lips to hers.

Doing this all alone would have been so much less interesting than doing this with her.

She blinked suddenly, like waking up from a trance, and turned away, letting go of him to resume her pacing along the edge of the meadow. "What are we going to do?"

He stood for a moment, looking at his empty hands. He had to think for a second about what she was really talking about. Layne. This amulet.

"I'd just as soon walk away. Like messing with high explosives, we don't need that shit."

A tiny, reflexive scowl crossed her lips. She never said anything about it, but hard swearing grated on her antique sensibilities. He figured he'd have her swearing just as bad, sooner or later.

"Look at it this way, then," she said. "Do you really want someone like Anderson Layne in possession of such a powerful magical artifact?"

No, no he didn't. Wasn't too long ago he would have figured it wasn't his problem, one way or another. Wasn't his business.

"It's exactly your business," Amelia argued. Cormac shouldn't have been surprised the thought slipped out. Or, she knew him well enough at this point to guess exactly what he was thinking. "Maybe you can't go out hunting rogue werewolves with silver bullets the way your father did, but you can do this. You may be the only one who can. What do you say to that?"

"I say you really want that amulet for yourself," he said.

She seemed taken aback a moment, straightening and studying him. Then, she smiled. "Well, yes. But that doesn't mean we won't do a world of good in the course of getting it."

He wasn't usually in the business of doing good. No, that wasn't true—that was how he'd justified every one of the kills he'd made. It was for the greater good, taking monsters out of the world. That was the job his father had given him. And whatever else he was, Anderson Layne was a certain kind of monster.

She stood tall with the strength of her convictions. "We're stronger than Kuzniak. It won't kill us."

"We're missing something."

"You're being cautious."

"Yes. Yes, I am."

"But you'll do it. You'll go after Layne and whatever this power is?"

He looked over his imaginary meadow and sighed. "Yeah."

* * *

He made the call. Barreling straight ahead without thinking too much about it, just like the old days. Layne answered after the first ring.

"Heard you wanted to talk to me," Cormac said, casually.

"That's right," Layne said, cautious, rightfully so. "I figured we had some stuff to work out. We can come to an understanding."

The guy wanted to shoot him dead on sight. "You want Kuzniak's book back, I got it. Do you even know what to do with it?"

"That's not the point."

Cormac could just keep poking at him until he got so angry he hung up. But that wasn't the goal here. "No, it's not; you know why? Because the book's not important. You've got something else. It killed Milo Kuzniak, and now you want to use it on me, isn't that right?"

Silence. That was the trick to handling a guy like Layne—keep him off balance, so he never knew how much you knew, or how strong you were. Cormac's reputation was going to carry him through this, if nothing else.

Cormac continued, "Do you even know what you have, or have you just been hanging on and hoping for the best?"

"You don't know anything, you're just mouthing off. I don't know why everyone's so scared of you.

You were never all that badass, it was all your dad. You're not half what your dad was."

Nobody even remembered his father. They only knew the image of him, the myth. He was twenty years dead and didn't have any power anymore.

If Cormac could flush the guy out right, maybe he could get him to just give it up. "Layne. I know you don't realize it, but you're way out of your league here. Why don't you just hand the thing over to me and I'll keep it safe."

"Yeah, right. Tell you what—you want the cross so bad, you come and take it from me." He spoke with a smugness that set Cormac's hair on end. He was missing something. "I'll meet you tonight. Midnight."

Damn theatrics. Why did magicians always have to do this shit at midnight?

You must admit, it is atmospheric.

"Fine," Cormac said. "Your place? You get it cleaned up good enough for company?"

"Let's go where this all got started. The old mining claim. You know it."

A place already saturated with old magic soaked into the ground. Not exactly neutral territory. But at least it was out in the open. "Fine," he said.

Layne was talking fast, angry. "And no guns, Cormac. You don't bring any guns, I won't bring any. Just you and me. Got it? We'll take care of this."

"I don't need guns, Layne." He hung up.

I appreciate how you trust my abilities so much that you don't even question if I'm capable of facing Anderson Layne in such a duel.

"Well, are you?"

I believe so. Yes.

She certainly sounded confident enough. He'd never doubted her.

Chapter 23

CORMAC MISSED his guns. The feel of them, the weight, the confidence they brought, the reassurance of his own power. He would reach under his jacket for a shoulder holster that wasn't there, purely out of habit, and feel off balance. Go for the gun at his hip and grab empty space instead. He always would, he thought. Slowly, he stopped missing the actual ability to shoot. Because Amelia brought her own firepower to the partnership.

The first time he'd seen her use magic in a fight was in prison, against a ravaging demon. The only thing that *could* defeat that monster had been magic. Bullets sure wouldn't have done it. She prevailed again, going up against some weather magician who had it in for Kitty. She explained the principles to him—was happy to explain—how one studied energies that already existed and worked to turn them, to use them against the person attacking, to build your own energy that you could use to defend yourself; that the world was made up of energy as much as it was made of matter and just because you couldn't see it didn't mean it wasn't there. Among the twentieth-century reading she'd been catching up on, she'd been very interested in quantum mechanics, because she said it sounded so much like how she thought of magic.

If he thought about it too hard, he'd shut down. The implications were too big. He didn't need to know how it worked, only that it did, and that he could use it when he needed to get himself out of trouble or make his intentions known in as decisive a manner as possible. So far, they'd done pretty well.

They had a couple of hours before they needed to hit the road, and Amelia spent that time reviewing the spells she thought she'd need and gathering the materials she'd use to work them. Not as simple as grabbing your revolver and checking the chamber, but what did he know? There might be demons.

He was on the freeway, halfway to Manitou, when he decided to call Kitty. Just in case something happened. Her phone rang once and went to voice mail. He clicked off the call rather than leave a message. A message wouldn't have made any sense and would be too late anyway.

It's Friday night, Cormac.

"Dammit," he muttered. Kitty's cell phone was off

because it was Friday night and she was at the KNOB studio doing her show.

You could call Ben. . . .

He was not up to the lecture he'd get from Ben, and he couldn't call Ben without telling him he was headed to a midnight showdown with Anderson Layne. Not that Kitty wouldn't lecture him, but the lecture would somehow be easier to take from her.

Because you don't have a lifetime of history with Kitty. When Kitty says you're being reckless, you tell yourself she doesn't know what she's talking about and that she's just being shrill. When Ben says you're being reckless, you can't ignore him because he knows you very, very well. And he's usually right.

"Whose side are you on?"

What a silly question that is.

He turned on the Jeep's radio and tuned it to KNOB. Her voice—rather, a more brash and manic version of her voice, her on-air personality—came through the speakers.

"—and what did you *think* would happen, when you invited your vampire boyfriend to your parents' house for dinner without telling them he's a vampire!"

A panicky-sounding woman answered. "That was the whole point of the dinner, to tell them that he's a vampire! I figured it was the best way, if they could actually see him—"

"And your boyfriend agreed to this?"

"I—I—I told him they already knew."

"So your Italian mother fixes a giant batch of garlicky pasta sauce that the vampire *can't eat,* and you wonder why everyone's mad at you?"

Listening to Kitty's show was like driving past a car wreck—you couldn't turn away.

"My mother hasn't spoken to me since, and Gerald says that maybe we should take some time off from things, and this isn't how I wanted things to turn out *at all*—"

"Then maybe you should have been up front with everyone in the first place. Boyfriends, parents, family dinners—this is primal stuff, you can't screw around with it. You definitely can't use these things as a hammer to passive-aggressively bludgeon everyone into thinking and feeling what you want them to."

"But—"

"I want you to practice something for me. Repeat these words: I'm sorry."

"But—"

"Say it. 'I'm sorry.'"

"I'm sorry?"

"You need to apologize to your mother, and your boyfriend. And none of this 'I'm sorry you were offended' crap. You need to be sorry that you lied to your boyfriend and that you didn't tell your mother that she probably shouldn't cook a big meal for this particular gathering."

"But all I did was make a little mistake—"

"Exactly! Apologizing is what we do after we make mistakes!"

The Midnight Hour's audience often seemed to call in wanting validation. Wanting to be told that they're right and everyone else in the world is wrong. Didn't usually work out for them, and Kitty had a great talent for cutting through their bullshit.

Kitty continued: "Here's the thing, and this goes for everyone out there: if having a boyfriend you can take home to meet your parents is important to you, and your parents are very traditional, then maybe you shouldn't date vampires. Trust me, I've had experience with this sort of thing."

Cormac had not met Kitty's parents, or her sister and her family. He had no intention of meeting them, because it would be too weird. What would he say? Hi, I met Kitty when I tried to kill her, and I had a thing for her for a while, but now we're just friends, but there still might be some feelings, and what? No. This was another reason she was better off with Ben, who went to her parents' house for dinner on a regular basis. He was a lawyer, he could talk about his job. He knew how to make small talk.

Cormac had the number for Kitty's direct line at the studio, one that would bypass the screening queue and go directly to her monitor. Which meant he shouldn't have gotten a busy signal when he called, but he did.

"Next caller, you're on the air, what have you got for me?"

"Hi, Kitty, longtime listener, thanks so much for taking my call, I just want to know what you think about vampire couples adopting children. Since they, you know, can't biologically have kids, do you think it's reasonable for them to want to adopt? And, you know, would you expect them to turn that child into a vampire when it got old enough? You know how some people say 'Don't you wish they could stay little forever?' Do you know if anyone's ever actually made their baby a vampire, to keep it from growing up?"

Maybe a third of the people who called in needed serious advice and made reasonable contributions to the discussion. The rest of her callers were like this: people who didn't know what the fuck they were talking about but sure had a lot of crazy going on.

Kitty sounded like she was in physical pain when she answered. He pictured her with her eyes closed, head in her hands. "There's so much wrong with everything you said that I don't even know where to start. First off, when we talk about vampire Families, we're not talking Mom and Dad and two-point-five kids. In all my years, I've never met a vampire who has expressed an interest in having children—some of them have had children *before* becoming vampires, and continue to care deeply for those children. But those children are usually already grown. I've never met a vampire with, you know, *children* children. Mostly because I imagine arranging day care would be a bitch. Also, I've never met a non-adult vampire. Doesn't mean they don't exist. I imagine it's possible. But you do know that people who wish babies could stay little forever are crazy, right? As the proud aunt of two adorable rugrats myself, I was so happy when they got to be old enough to take *themselves* to the restroom, you know? Anyway. From a purely biological perspective, vampires don't reproduce by having children, they reproduce by infecting others with vampirism. . . ."

He tried her number again, and again. The third call got through, and a man's flat, professional voice answered. "You've reached *The Midnight Hour.* What's your question or comment?"

The screener. Somehow, the direct line had shunted him over to her regular call-in line. She didn't have a screener in the early days of her show. She'd gotten a lot bigger since then. His frustration grew.

"It's Matt, isn't it?" he said. "I thought this was the direct line—I need to talk to Kitty, now."

"Who's this?" the guy said. "Where are you calling from?"

"Just put me through to Kitty."

"You can't just talk to Kitty, she's in the middle of—"

"It's Cormac. She'll talk to me. Put me through."

"No! Wait a minute, Cormac—aren't you that guy who wanted to kill her?"

People kept harping on that. He'd never live it down. "Tell her I'm on the line."

"I don't think—"

"Just do it." He did not have the patience for this shit. "Tell her it's important."

"Please hold," Matt spat at him. He probably didn't have the patience either, but at least he had a button to push to pass the buck. "And you'll need to turn your radio off."

He did. He knew Kitty had a monitor, that she picked what calls to answer based on the screener's listing. He wanted Matt to just *tell* her he was on the line. The lack of control was aggravating.

Then Kitty picked up. He was kind of surprised. "Cormac. What the hell?"

"What happened to your direct line?"

"Wait, what?"

"Your direct line, the emergency number—"

She groaned. "We've been having problems since we added a couple more lines. I'm sorry. I'll get Matt to look at it after the show. Wait a minute . . . are you having an emergency?"

Was he? Probably. "No. I just need to tell you something."

"Can't it wait? I'm in the middle of the show!"

"Yeah. I'm kind of in the middle of something, too; it can't wait."

"Maybe I can make us both happy—can I put you on the air? Just for a couple of—"

"No. Hell no."

"Just a couple of questions, people will love it!"

"Kitty—"

"Please?"

He sighed. Why did he even bother? "Fine."

You really are a big softy at heart, aren't you? Amelia said teasingly.

Yeah, or something.

A sound in the background clicked and the quality of the line changed to a more open tone, with more interference.

Sure enough, her next words were, "And I've got a sudden visit from a special guest. My very longtime listeners will know exactly who I'm talking about. It's my great pleasure to introduce sometime bounty hunter and man of mystery, Cormac. Cormac, welcome!"

He ought to just hang up on her. "Norville. Make it quick."

"Right. So, Cormac, what have you been up to since the last time we talked?"

He didn't say a word. Not necessarily because he was trying to be difficult. He just couldn't think of anything he'd want to say to Kitty's nationwide audience.

Kitty only let the dead air linger for a second or two. "I think I've mentioned that Cormac is the strong and silent type, yes? Maybe he'll be up for a game of twenty questions. Cormac, twenty questions, yes or no."

"No," he stated.

"Are you on a job right now?"

He wasn't entirely sure how to answer that. Or if he should. "Yes. And I need to talk to you about it. *Privately.*"

"I can't believe this, I'm being coerced on my own show. You know you're one of the few people who could get away with this," she muttered. "All right, don't go anywhere, because after a short break for local messages, we'll get right back to your calls on *The Midnight Hour.*"

He listened closely for the click and change in tone that meant they were off the air. Not that he didn't trust her, but the reassurance was nice.

"Cormac, what are you doing?" she said.

"If something happens to me, if something goes wrong, you need to go to Judi and Frida and tell them you know how Milo Kuzniak killed Crane. It's a spell attached to some kind of Maltese cross amulet. Tell them that, and get them to help you with Amy Scanlon's book."

"What do you mean, if something happens to you? Why can't you tell them yourself?"

"Nothing's going to go wrong. I'm going after that amulet and I have to go through some not-very-nice people to get it. It'll be fine."

"Except, just in case, you had to tell me? Because you're meeting not-very-nice people at midnight? There is nothing about this situation that sounds not-dangerous."

"Amelia's looking out for me."

"No offense, but that doesn't reassure me."

"You trust me or not?"

She didn't say anything, which he supposed was the best he could expect in response to that question.

"You know I'm going to call Ben right after this, right?"

"Better it comes from you than me."

"That's so dysfunctional. Do you even listen to the show? You know how many problems come from people not telling each other things?"

"Kitty—"

"Call me when it's all over. Let me know everything's fine."

"I'll call." He hung up before she could say anything else.

"Dysfunctional" is one of those eminently useful modern words that serves as a catchall for so many

otherwise complicated issues. It tends to lose meaning, doesn't it?

"Well. She's not wrong."

Amelia didn't argue.

Chapter 24

HE DIDN'T park in the same turnout; he figured Layne would have someone watching it and wouldn't be above just shooting him as he stepped out of the car. Instead, he parked a couple of miles away and left himself enough time to hike to the plateau. He had a flashlight, held it low and out to show his path, but otherwise preserved his night vision.

A wind was blowing, a front moving in. The overcast sky reflected ambient light from the city, giving the world a weird, shrouded glow. A bite in the air threatened snow. Another frustration to add to the list, since the weather forecasters couldn't decide if the storm was going to produce a mere dusting or a real blizzard. Didn't matter one way or another, but it would be nice to know what to expect. He could say that about his whole life, he supposed.

Cormac didn't see any other cars in the turnout; Layne must have had his own parking spot staked out. Cormac knew he couldn't get to the plateau first. Layne was closer and had a head start. The guy had the high ground, nothing Cormac could do about it. If Layne didn't shoot him as he left his car, he might lie in wait and shoot Cormac in the back as he made the climb.

He won't do that. He wants the standoff. He wants to face you and prove how powerful he is.

Either way, Cormac was going to be very careful.

And that's why we packed ahead of time.

She had a spell, one she'd wanted to use back when they made their foray at Layne's place, and she was gleeful to be using it now. This wasn't an amulet or a ritual like many of her other spells—this was a potion, ingredients mixed, boiled, infused in alcohol, and kept in a little perfume bottle. Saffron, dried hemlock, and powdered cuttlefish—which, shockingly, he'd been able to find at an Asian market downtown. Like the Maltese cross–shaped amulet that had brought them out here in the first place, this was more of a charm than a spell. No preparation or ritual needed, no saying the right words in the right order or drawing the right patterns. It was the kind of thing anyone could do, if they knew how. Charms and potions like this would have been passed down in families, from grandparents and parents to children, back when the world was darker and the shadows bigger. Amelia had learned it from an old woman in England's Lake District.

It seems to me the shadows are just as large as they've ever been. But people have forgotten to look for them.

Or new shadows replaced the old. A person could only worry about so many things at a time.

Let's just worry about the next hour, yes?

One step at a time, same as it had always been.

He poured out a single drop of the potion, used it to anoint himself, a circle on his forehead. And that was that. Walking through the nighttime woods with the charm in place didn't feel any different than walking without it. He'd expected invisibility magic to act like a cloak, muffling his senses, making the world indistinct around him even as it made him indistinct to the world. Or maybe he watched too many movies.

The charm doesn't confer invisibility. That's very powerful magic, too much to waste on this. This—it simply involves perception. It encourages observers to look away. They don't see you, not because you're invisible, but because they don't see you.

Magic by semantics. Sure, why not?

He stopped hiking when he heard something. Snap of a twig, a rustle against a tree branch, a murmured voice. Layne brought friends. The voices only spoke a word or two, but they seemed to be looking for someone. Whoever was here, they hadn't seen him. Cormac moved as quietly as he could. When he reached the end of the deer path and emerged from the trees, the plateau opened before him, a dried-out stretch. The wind had stopped and the air was still. Sound carried, and he heard a pair of voices calling to each other in stifled whispers. They were among the trees, on the other side of the slope. He wiped his forehead, erasing the spell's mark, and waited.

"Hey! Where'd he come from!"

"I thought you were watching!"

Layne's two goons emerged from the trees across the flat space, staring at him, their jaws dropped. They had guns in holsters but hadn't drawn yet. Whether things stayed that way depended on how much control Layne actually had over them.

Layne himself moved up from behind them to the middle of the plateau, hands at his sides. He wore a sly smile.

"Wasn't sure you'd actually have the guts to show up," he said, a predictable bit of bluster. Cormac smirked back.

Flakes of snow started falling, picturesque white spots drifting slowly, as if independent of gravity.

Oh my goodness. I've read about gunfights at high noon in the Old West. I never thought to see one.

You ready to draw, then? Cormac asked her.

I don't know. I don't like the way he's smiling at us, as if he knows something we don't.

That's the mind game. He's being intimidating, trying to throw us off. I'm doing the same thing. Remember, winning a shootout isn't about just being fast, it's about being accurate.

I'm not sure I can—

You've done this before. Against the demon, against Harold Franklin.

But that's just it, I knew exactly what they could do, exactly where they drew their powers from. I knew what spells to use against them. This—we only have one chance, and I don't know the right spell. We still don't know what the amulet does, only that it exists.

The answer popped into his head—you use the strongest one, of course. Just like you used the most powerful weapon you had, and you hit as hard as you could. Make sure you only need to strike once and don't give the enemy a chance to stand back up.

Amelia knew what offensive spell was her strongest; he felt her confidence. The storm helped; she could chant a phrase and use a talisman to call lightning out of the overcast sky. Fry Layne where he stood. Cormac sort of looked forward to it. At her direction, he found the right talisman, a Thor's hammer in his left-hand jacket pocket. She could invoke storm magic from a half a dozen cultures, use the energies already brewing above them to strike a blow.

Remember, he told her, you're a more experienced magician than he is. He doesn't know what the hell he's doing.

But what if he doesn't have to?

The comment made him pause, and he tilted his head as if listening. Quickly he brought his gaze back to Layne, and wondered what the other man made of the gesture. Only a handful of people knew about Amelia. To everyone else, Cormac had just suddenly become a powerful magician. Part of the legend, right?

The snow remained scant, occasional flakes rather than a real snowfall. Not enough to interfere with his line of sight. But the clouds thickened, billows like cotton batting gathering overhead. His hair stood on end, from static cracking in the air.

Layne stood like a man invincible, who could not fail. He knows something, Cormac thought.

Amelia had retreated into herself, pondering. Cormac nudged her.

What if he doesn't have to do anything? she repeated. *A powerful offense is unnecessary if your defensive capabilities are strong enough. What if, what if . . .*

"I thought you were badass, Bennett! Show me what you've got!"

He's provoking us. He wants us to attack.

It did seem that way. He'd set some kind of trap, and if they attacked him outright, they'd walk right into it. Cormac was raised to be a hunter; he was a patient man. The longer he stood and glared at Layne, the more flustered the man would get. He had time. More important that they figure this out.

Blue and white streaks of light flashed in the clouds, lightning waiting to be summoned. All Amelia had to do was say the word and call down a bolt to smash Layne.

He's not a magician, Amelia said, her thoughts racing. *All he has is the amulet.*

That was it. The key to it all.

"I've got it," he murmured, at the same time Amelia realized, *I've got it.*

That was what the amulet was, what it did—somehow, it used a magician's attack against him. The original Milo Kuzniak didn't have any magical ability, just smoke and mirrors and a notebook filled with folklore, but when Augustus Crane attacked, he died. And when the younger Milo Kuzniak attacked, he died.

It's a mirror. The amulet is reflective. I call down lightning on Layne, I'd only be calling it down on myself. I can't do anything to him, Cormac. Through him, she made a gesture, dropped the Thor's hammer back in his pocket. The static charge in the air dissipated, the lightning overhead faded. He breathed out like he'd just left a minefield.

Well then, he thought, I guess it's up to me. He started walking.

Amelia said, *We'll need to take care of those men with guns.*

Give them a light show, a flash or a bang or something. Won't need much to scare them off.

Fortunately, she'd brought along some of her reliable standbys—one of them was a thumb-sized quartz crystal, charged with magic to give off brilliant light. And simple, non-magical packs of gunpowder, good for making noise. Surprising, how much of this was just stagecraft.

Layne's eyes widened in surprise, and Cormac kept his slow pace forward, his gaze focused. His grin showed annoyance.

One of the henchmen called out, "Layne—Layne what's going on, you want us to—"

"Just hold it," Layne called back, brusque and clearly nervous. His hands flexed at his sides, as if reaching for a gun. Regular Old West gunfighter. To Cormac he said, "You better watch it. You don't want to end up dead like Kuzniak, do you? You watch it, Bennett, wait a minute—"

When he was just shy of arm's reach, Cormac moved fast, left hand flashing out to grab Layne's collar while his right hand punched hard into his nose.

Layne choked out a cry and tried to stumble back, but Cormac kept hold of his shirt, keeping the guy upright while he stepped in for a hard knee into the groin that dropped him like a rock. This time, Cormac let him fall. Kicked him in the gut for good measure, then fell on him, putting a knee in his back, twisting his arm to immobilize him.

"Layne!" His guys called out, but it had happened so fast they were dumbstruck.

Keeping hold of Layne with one hand, he reached into his pocket for the quartz, which he threw straight up. It lit up with the glow of a sun, a flash like a bomb going off. There were a couple of shouts and screams, and the sound of a couple of grown men tearing through the underbrush, fleeing as if chased by devils.

Cormac gave Layne's arm an extra twist and waited a moment to see if he was going to struggle. He didn't. The guy's face was smashed into the ground, and his breath came out in crying wheezes.

That, Amelia said. *That was* lovely.

The plateau had gone still. The snow was already slacking off. Just a late winter flurry. Kind of peaceful. Cormac wanted to get the hell out of here. Get inside, get warm, have a drink.

He searched Layne's pockets, jeans and coat, and found it in the inside coat pocket. Spared little more than a glimpse at it—a Maltese cross, a couple of inches across, made of highly polished bronze, exactly the right size and shape to match the imprint in the book—before slipping it in his own pocket.

He slammed Layne's face into the ground to stun him before getting up and backing off.

Slowly, Layne rolled to his back. Blood ran down his face from a couple of wounds, a scrape on his forehead and a cut lip. Not to mention that smashed nose. He curled around his gut, moaning in pain and swearing with every breath.

Some coherent phrases broke through. "You can't take that! That's mine! It's *mine*!"

He was beat up, not broken, and his guys would crawl back to check on him soon enough. All Cormac had to do was be gone before they got brave. He was done here.

"Some advice," Cormac said. "There's no gold up here, or if there is you aren't going to get it out with magic. Magic's not going to make you rich, and it won't make you strong. You mess around with it long enough, it'll make you dead. Especially if you don't know what the hell you're doing. Go back to your black market and your drug running or whatever the hell it is you're doing. And leave me alone."

Layne didn't say anything, just lay there groaning, spitting curses. Cormac walked away.

Chapter 25

HE WAS glad for the couple of miles of walking. Gave him a chance to burn off the adrenaline and a bad case of nerves. He stretched the hand he'd used to punch Layne; it was sore, but not busted. The skin was scraped up. He was tingling all over, fight response still burning through him, waiting for the next blow. The walk gave his heart a chance to slow down.

Amelia was quiet. Maybe thinking hard like he was, about what would have happened if they'd kept going, brought down that lightning spell on Layne's head—and had it strike them instead. It wouldn't even have looked like murder, just an unlucky bit of chance, getting struck by lightning in the foothills. Accidental, however mysterious, just like the other deaths. The perfect weapon in a wizards' duel—the one no one even knew was there.

When he reached the Jeep, he wasn't done moving. He drove east for a while, out of the hills and to the plains, flat scrubby farmland covered by a dusting of new snow. Dawn was breaking by then, the overcast sky going pale. He stopped, pulled over, sat there watching the sky get lighter through the windshield, until the gray clouds turned pink with the rising sun, and the snow in the fields sparkled, crystalline with ice. The sun itself broke over the horizon, an unreal shape burning orange, peering through a clear space for ten or fifteen minutes before disappearing behind clouds.

It's beautiful.

He agreed. But he also thought, of course. He took it for granted that a sunrise was beautiful. Just like sunsets. And the mountains, a bull elk walking through a morning mist, a hawk soaring on the hunt. It hardly needed mentioning.

Are you ready to look at what we won, then?

He found the amulet in the pocket where he'd shoved it. In the morning light, they finally had a chance to study it.

The thing was simply crafted, with only moderate skill. The bronze cross shape had a lead border soldered around the edges, roughly done, bubbles and irregularities visible in spots. A wire loop had been soldered on. The bronze itself was clean, polished, front and back. When he held it up, he could see his reflection, a wavery, yellow-tinged version of himself.

It's a mirror, literally, Amelia said. *In ancient*

times, before mirrors made with silver-painted glass came about, people used polished brass or bronze. I believe this is very old, Cormac.

Where do you suppose Milo Kuzniak got it?

Haven't any idea. Boggles the mind, doesn't it?

Of course it did. That was what all this was for, boggling the mind.

I could scry. See if there's any mention in the usual arcane literature of this sort of spell—or perhaps even the existence of this specific amulet, though I think that's unlikely.

He started the Jeep and put it into gear.

May I ask where we're going?

"Manitou Springs. To see Judi and Frida. This thing's a red herring. I want to get back to cracking Amy's book of shadows."

But— She stopped. Didn't argue.

Cormac kept driving, west this time, back to town.

THEY GOT to the Manitou Wishing Well before it opened. On the plus side, there was plenty of parking on the street right out front. He found a coffee shop nearby and bought the biggest coffee they had and a Danish. Enough fuel to keep him going for a couple more hours. He watched the tourist stretch wake up for the day, lights coming on and shops opening, until Judi came to the window and turned the hand-painted sign hung on the door from CLOSED to OPEN.

No point in waiting.

He walked in, found Judi restocking T-shirts and Frida sorting receipts by the cash register. They stared at him and seemed surprised to see him.

He stalked to the counter by Frida, put down the mirror amulet, and turned to face them. Judi had drifted over; they both stared. Esther the cat thudded onto the far end of the counter, curled her tail around her, and blinked calmly at him. Cormac looked at her, sidelong, suspicious, before launching in on it.

"Milo Kuzniak didn't kill Augustus Crane. Not outright. He probably didn't know much magic at all, but he had this. Crane killed himself. He went out there to get rid of Kuzniak, and whatever spell he used doubled back and killed him instead. Not sure what exactly this is, what kind of magic is tangled up in it, but it's some kind of reflective spell. Murder solved. And the bad guys you were worried about? I don't think they'll be poking around anymore."

He leaned on the counter, regarding them, and waited for a response. He seemed to have startled them, which was okay. He'd wait.

Frida pointed at the glass. "Could you not lean on that? I just cleaned it."

Cormac crossed his arms.

Judi finally nodded. "Right. Okay. That makes sense." She picked up the amulet. Turned it back and forth in the light. It seemed so harmless, a junk-store trinket. "This little thing? Are you sure?"

"Pretty sure." No need to tell them it had been used to kill another man recently. "That it? Was this what you needed to know?"

The two women looked at each other, exchanging some silent reassurance.

Frida said, "How did you find this? We could never find anything."

"It took some luck. I had a few contacts. Turned out, Milo Kuzniak's great-grandson had it. He was following in his ancestor's footsteps, trying to get gold out of that plateau." He gave a little shrug.

"Great-grandson?" she said, astonished.

Wasn't any more unbelievable than anything else about this story.

Frida said, "Then it's all just this? Whatever lingering magic is up there, it's not a danger to anyone?"

"I don't think so. It's all shadows anymore."

"Thank you," Judi breathed, wondering. She replaced the amulet on the counter, gingerly, as if it had burned her.

Cormac asked, "So—you have the key to Amy's book? Am I worthy?"

He thought she might back out of the deal, or that she had been lying about knowing how to read the book. He expected her to say she didn't know, and he didn't know how he was going to deal with it. Not like he could beat up a couple of old women like he beat up Layne.

But Judi nodded, moving around the counter to the back room. "Of course. I'll go get it."

That left him face-to-face with Frida, who regarded him with bemusement.

"I didn't think you'd find anything," she said. "I figured we'd never see you again. I mostly suggested it to try to get rid of you."

That was fair, the mistrust being mutual. "What's in Amy's book—it's too important to just let go. I wasn't going to walk away."

"I see that now."

Cormac pushed the amulet across to her. "I figure this is yours. You hired me to find out what happened—this is it."

Frida regarded it as if it were on fire. Donning a wry smile, she pushed it back. "No, you keep it. I have a feeling you'll need it more than we ever will."

It was a hot potato, then, and he didn't want anything to do with it. It was Amelia who reached for it and said, "I might just at that," as she slipped it in a jacket pocket.

The cat yawned, showing a mouth full of teeth, and bounded off the counter and away.

Judi returned with a tiny hardcover journal, no bigger than a credit card. Another damned book. She flipped through the pages, smiling fondly, stroking the edge of the cover. A last connection to the dead. A farewell.

She explained, "It was a code we worked out together, just the two of us, when she was in high school. She didn't want anyone to know what she was getting into, but she knew I'd understand. I'm the one who set her on this path, after all. For good or ill." If she had regrets, she hid them well, behind a simple sad smile and a serene gaze.

She's wise, Amelia said. *She shouldn't blame herself. She couldn't have known what Amy would do. Amy followed her own path in the end. Like I did.*

"It's a substitution cipher. It's a different key for every page, and each page will mark what key to use. The code's not totally unbreakable, but it's rather difficult because we based it on syllables, not letters. Here's the key."

She handed him the little book. It felt like taking hold of someone's soul. Maybe it was—Amy's heart, her intentions, scribbled in lines of writing and symbols. He flipped through a few pages. It didn't make any more sense than her book did, but he recognized the symbols, and there was a repetitive quality to it—symbols, and what they meant—that could be applied to the book of shadows.

This make sense to you? he questioned Amelia.

Oh, yes. This will do nicely. Give me a little time,

I'll have it. They seemed to have converted English to a syllabic script, then encrypted the text. A rather lovely system.

He put the book in his pocket before she could get too involved. "Thank you," Cormac said, heartfelt.

"This isn't just idle curiosity," Judi said. "You need this for something. You're on some kind of quest."

"More like fighting a battle," he said. "Amy's book might have just what we need to win."

Judi asked, "This battle—who are you fighting against? How bad is it?"

How to explain in just a few words? The things he'd seen, the battles he'd already fought—he couldn't explain. Not without sounding crazy. Not without scaring them.

"It's pretty bad," he said.

"Oh. Well. Good luck, then," she said.

He gave a wave and walked out of the shop.

Chapter 26

AMELIA WORKED for a week, printed pages from the grimoire on one side of the table, blank sheets where she deciphered the writing on the other. The stack of deciphered pages grew. For now, she didn't worry about reading them, about picking apart the meaning. Just get it all translated, then read. Cormac had to force her to take breaks; she might have been disembodied, but he had to eat and sleep.

What they initially gleaned from Amy's spellbook: She had written about the lore she encountered, the spells and rituals, and poured out her thoughts about what they meant, how they might have developed, and how she might use them. This was before she met Kumarbis. After she met Kumarbis, she wrote what she learned from him. The stories he told her, the spells he taught her. Her tone became starstruck early on, as she grew enamored of the sheer weight of history behind him—he'd existed for more than three thousand years, Kitty estimated. Amy wanted to be a part of the story. She embraced his quest and did what she could to solve the puzzle of what he was trying to do—exactly how, once the vampire had collected enough allies and power, he was going to assert himself on the world and defeat Roman. Kumarbis knew everything about Roman—up to a point. Amy had tried to examine everything about that point she could. The trouble was, Kumarbis simply didn't know everything about Roman, Dux Bellorum. Once the two had gone their separate ways, Kumarbis was cut off.

It could have been me, Amelia observed, nearing the end of her decoding. *If Kumarbis had found me in Istanbul or Baghdad or any of the other cities I spent time in, I'd have been just as starstruck. I'd have followed him just as eagerly as Amy did, so I could learn more. Learn everything. Perhaps we do have much in common.*

The whole thing made Cormac a little bit sad.

When Cormac had some kind of handle on the narrative and the information it held, he called Kitty.

"Oh my God," she said, before *hello* even. "Why haven't you been answering your phone?"

"I've been busy," he said curtly.

"Well yeah, obviously, but you can't at least check in once in a while?"

"Were you worried about me?"

He heard amusement in her voice. "I only worry

when I get calls from the police about you." Well. That was fair. "And Ben drove by your apartment and saw your Jeep parked there, and he said that probably meant you were working and you'd call when you were good and ready."

Also fair. Made him nervous sometimes, how well Ben knew him. Nervous, and lucky.

"We have to talk," he said. "I got the key to decoding Amy's book, and I think I found something."

She paused a moment, then said, "You should probably come over."

HE ARRIVED at their house and found a home-cooked dinner waiting. He felt another one of those moments of displacement. On the one hand, this wasn't him, this house in the suburbs and dinner with glasses of wine and actual domesticity; on the other hand, he could get used to it. It left him standing at the edge of the kitchen, bundle of papers under his arm, torn in two directions.

Amelia nudged him to say "*thank you*" and take his seat at the table to share in salad and pasta marinara. By unspoken agreement, they waited until after food to talk. Even so, Kitty still had food on her plate when she leaned forward, eyes wide, and asked, "Well?"

"Where should I start?" Cormac asked. The story was a tangle that he was still working out.

"Start with the hundred-and-fifteen-year-old murder," Ben asked. "You didn't actually figure it out, did you?"

"I believe I did," Cormac answered smugly, and told a trimmed-down version of the whole thing. He left out the parts where he committed arson, failed to report a suspicious death to the proper authorities, and beat the crap out of Anderson Layne. By the skeptical looks on their faces, he was pretty sure Ben and Kitty guessed he was leaving out details. They were smart enough not to push him.

"And Judi gave you the key, just like that?" Kitty said.

"Whole code, all laid out."

"So she could have helped you all along."

He said, "I think they wanted to make sure I was serious. That I wasn't just screwing around."

"So it really was a test like in a fairy tale." Kitty wrinkled her nose.

"Whatever it was—the key worked. Amelia decoded the whole thing." He thumbed the stack of pages he'd brought. He figured Kitty would appreciate the reading. "I also asked your Web guy to take down the online version. Figure we didn't need it hanging around anymore."

"And . . . what?" she said, and sure enough she was reaching for the stack with curved, clawlike fingers. "You find anything? Did she say anything?"

He could sit there with half a grin on his face and drive her nuts, but he didn't. He had the page folded down, the one where Amy explained why Kumarbis dedicated himself to destroying Roman, and drew it out to hand to Kitty.

Her eyes scanned over the lines, written in Amelia's pointed cursive, and she started reading out loud.

"'So amazing, thinking that such a power might exist. And yet utterly chilling. Kumarbis, for all his vague notions, for all his damaged psyche, is right—even if Dux Bellorum did nothing else, what he did at Herculaneum means he is viciously dangerous and must be stopped.'"

"Herculaneum?" Ben said. "What's that have to do with anything?"

Cormac said, "Herculaneum is another town buried by the eruption of Vesuvius that destroyed Pompeii."

"I know, but what does it have to do—"

"Wait. Be quiet, I have to think." Kitty put up her hand, scrunched up her face, held her head as if she could squeeze the memory out. "It was something Kumarbis said, but it was right before everything went to hell. It's all a mess . . . I can't remember." She opened her eyes wide. "Herculaneum. When I asked him about the Manus Herculei, that artifact Roman was going after, he said it didn't refer to Hercules, it was Herculaneum. I just remember thinking, what the hell is that? Then I had other things to deal with." Her thoughts darkened, turned inward. The trauma surfaced, sometimes. But she buried it quickly.

Ben was the one who broke the heavy silence. "Wait—so we are saying that Roman used magic to cause the eruption of Vesuvius? That's the implication here, right?"

Because this wasn't the first time Cormac and Amelia had been presented with that possibility, they weren't surprised.

"Could he do it again?" Kitty asked softly.

That was the implication. They still weren't any closer to finding Roman or knowing how to stop him.

Ben said, "So, what, we need a geologist on the team now? We can't guard every active volcano on the planet. Even if he was able to make a volcano explode, why would he do it? What would it accomplish? Who's to say he didn't just, I don't know, hate Pompeii?"

Kitty reached for the bottle of wine to pour another glass, but it was empty. She sighed. "I'll spread the word. I'll let everyone know what we've found. Maybe the old vampires like Marid can shed some light on things. Um, no pun intended." She considered her empty glass of wine and furrowed her brow.

Meanwhile, Ben had gone to the cupboard to fetch another bottle, and he refilled Kitty's glass. Cormac shook his head at the offer of more. He needed to hit the road soon.

He'd gone and solved a whole collection of mysteries, a hundred-year-old murder and a magician's secret code. He even got paid—even if it was Layne's dirty money. Still spent the same. He ought to feel satisfied. Instead, he had a nagging suspicion he was missing something.

CORMAC LAID them all out on his table at home: one of the mangled coins of Dux Bellorum, the first one that had belonged to Kumarbis himself; a pair of goggles with very dark glass and aged leather that once belonged to a demon who might very well have come from Hell; the USB drive that had belonged to Amy Scanlon, in its reliquary; and Milo Kuzniak's mirrored amulet, which didn't have anything to do with the others, but he might as well keep it with the rest of the trophies. The rest of the clues. Mysteries with loose ends hanging.

If only objects could talk, to find out where this had come from, who it had belonged to, and did the elder Kuzniak find it or steal it, and on and on. He still didn't have a way to look into the future to see what was coming next.

We could find a practitioner of psychometry—

No. It didn't matter, it wasn't important. What was important: looking forward.

The Long Game—it's bigger than the vampires, isn't it?

Likely. But he was betting the only vampire who knew that was Roman. He was manipulating the whole thing, gathering power, collecting spells and rituals, and it couldn't be for any good purpose.

He could walk away. This wasn't his fight.

But you won't. You can't.

Kitty and Ben wouldn't walk away. He wasn't in this to figure out what Roman was really up to and what he planned next. He was here to make sure they didn't get themselves killed or worse. That was good enough for him.

SINCE SOLVING the problem of Amy's book, he hadn't checked the e-mail tied to the online version, which the Webmaster had left active. Before heading to bed for the night, he looked and found unread messages waiting for him, including one from his learned correspondent. The one Amelia had a crush on.

Not a crush. Professional admiration.

Right, whatever you say. Cormac read the e-mail.

"I notice you removed Amy Scanlon's book from your Web site. I assume that means you successfully decoded it?"

He had a dilemma. He didn't want to say yes—that would show way too much of his hand, and this guy was way too interested. He typed out a carefully ambiguous response: "Still working on it, but I decided having it online wasn't solving anything."

Hard, not to sit there staring at the screen, waiting for a response. He was inclined to take a walk around the block, even this late at night, but Amelia suggested reading a book instead—a history of Pompeii and the eruption of Vesuvius. He kept glancing up at the screen.

It's the illusion of being instantaneous, Amelia complained. *It raises expectations intolerably.*

When the e-mail arrived, an hour or so later, the computer dinged its arrival.

The response read: "I would like to meet you. You have skills and knowledge, and I can use someone with both."

Well, that was interesting.

We are looking for employment, aren't we?

"That depends. I get the feeling this guy isn't offering employment, but something else."

You're nervous.

"You bet I am." He typed in a response: "I don't know anything about you. Who are you?"

They waited. The next message arrived.

"I am called Roman."

The words swam, then grew large. Coincidence. Maybe it was a coincidence.

Not fucking likely.

Cormac grit his teeth and raced to come up with a reply, because this was happening real time now and any pause would raise suspicions. He couldn't let on that he'd heard the name before, that he knew who his correspondent was. He ought to shut down communications entirely—but that would also raise suspicions. And this—it was too good a lead. If only he could figure out exactly what to say, the words that wouldn't make Roman suspect he was talking to an enemy. This had to sound ordinary, to make Roman complacent. Draw him in without bringing doom on himself. He'd never hunted anything like this.

I have good reason to believe that the eruption of Vesuvius that buried Pompeii was instigated by magic, the man had written before. Oh, Cormac just bet he did.

Tell him this, Amelia said.

Cormac typed out, "My name is Amelia Parker. Let's do meet." And hit SEND.

She was crazy. He never should have let her do that, but the words were already gone. On the other hand . . . They wanted to stop Roman—this was the best chance anyone had had to do it. Meet the guy, put a nice solid stake in his chest before he even knew what was happening. Done and done.

But I have so many questions. . . .

No. We stake this guy on sight, no hesitation.

Amelia didn't argue.

"Very good to meet you, Amelia Parker. I'll be in touch," the man called Roman replied. And that was that. Cormac didn't have anything to say after that.

He didn't know if Kitty was going to be happy about this, or kill him.

"YOU ENJOY it. The hunt, the anticipation," Amelia said.

"Not sure *enjoy* is the right word." It was a rush, a thrill. An addiction. Possibly the only thing he was good at.

She wore a thin smile, immensely satisfied at the work they'd done. Even the curveball at the end couldn't dull her enthusiasm. It was another mystery to chase, more knowledge to be won.

The meadow was sunny today. High summer, a haze hanging in the air, insects flitting above the creek. Nice contrast to the winter chill in the waking world. He could tip his face up, feel the sun, and never get a sunburn. They sat on their pair of rocks, close enough to touch if he wanted to.

"This could get us killed," he said. It was what he'd been thinking about. "Roman's seen me, he knows what I look like and who I am. If we really set up a meeting and go through with it, he'll know something's wrong. He won't give us a chance to say anything. It'll be another one of your gunfights at high noon."

"Or midnight, rather, considering what he is. You don't think we can win against him in a face-to-face meeting."

"He's two thousand years old and he's spent all that time getting more dangerous. I think we have a chance. Just not a very good one. I just want to make sure you're okay with that."

"You think because I so assiduously avoided death once, I'm loathe to face it again?" She pulled her knees up, tucked under her long skirt, and her gaze was downcast. "Of course I'd rather not face it again. I'm well aware that when you die, I likely will as well. I don't believe the fabric of my soul can survive that trial a second time. And it's your life, Cormac. It's your decision to make."

But it wasn't. Not entirely, not anymore. What a weird thought.

Amelia was watching him, studying him. "I'm sorry," she said.

"For what?"

"For being here. Your life would be very different, if not for me. I would hate to think that I've damaged you in some way. Altered what you would have been without me."

Good odds that what he would have been was dead. Or back in prison, or back to hunting and damn the consequences. He gave a wry smile. "You didn't much care about damaging me at the start."

"A lot's happened since then."

Yes, it had. What hadn't changed: even without the

guns, he kept getting in trouble and someday, somehow he was likely to get himself killed. It didn't scare him.

He said, "You being here means that whenever I die, however it happens, if it's going up against Roman or something else that gets us—I won't be alone."

He held out his hand to her, and she took it.

Award-winning authors
Compelling stories

Please join us at the website
below for more information
about this author and other great
Tor selections, and to sign up for
our monthly newsletter!